Walter Mosley is the author of eight books in the Easy Rawlins series, all published by Serpent's Tail: *Devil in a Blue Dress*, *A Red Death*, *White Butterfly*, *Black Betty*, *A Little Yellow Dog*, *Gone Fishin'*, *Bad Boy Brawly Brown* and *Six Easy Pieces*. His other works of fiction, also published by Serpent's Tail, are *RL's Dream*, *Blue Light*, *Always Outnumbered*, *Always Outgunned*, *Walkin' the Dog*, *Fearless Jones* and *Fear Itself*, and the non-fiction title, *What Next: A Memoir Toward World Peace*. He lives in New York.

Praise for
The Man in My Basement

'Confirms him as possibly the most important current American writer'

Time Out

'A philosophical inquiry about corruption, made real through Mosley's committed colloquialism and a willingness to debate without any final vote – this is never a parable, but rather a complex story of negotiating rage and self-loathing'

Times Literary Supplement

'Mosley makes this such a lucid, sinuous book that its big issues are handled with idiosyncratic grace... audacious, inventive book'

Scotsman

Other titles by Walter Mosley
published by Serpent's Tail

WALTER MOSLEY

The Man
in My Basement

The right of Walter Mosley to be identified as the author of this work has been
asserted by him in accordance with the Copyright, Designs and Patents Act 1988

Copyright © 2004 by Walter Mosley

First published in the USA by Little, Brown and Company,
Boston and New York in 2004

First published in the UK in 2004 by Serpent's Tail,
4 Blackstock Mews, London N4 2BT
website: www.serpentstail.com

First published in this 5-star edition in 2005

Printed by Mackays of Chatham, plc

10 9 8 7 6 5 4 3 2

For the man of the world, Harry Belafonte

PART ONE

PART ONE

one

"Mr. Blakey?" the small white man asked.

I had answered the door expecting big Clarance Mayhew and his cousin Ricky. The three of us had a standing date to play cards on Thursday nights. I was surprised even to hear the doorbell because it was too early for my friends to have made it home from work and neither one of them would have rung the bell anyway. We'd been friends since childhood, since my grandparents owned the house.

"My house is your house," I always said to Clarance and Ricky. I never locked the door because we lived in a secluded colored neighborhood way back from the highway. Everybody knows everybody in my neighborhood, so strangers don't go unnoticed. If somebody stole something from me, I'd have known who it was, what kind of car he drove, and the numbers on his license plate before he was halfway to Southampton.

"Yes," I said to the small, bald-headed white man in the dark-green suit. "I'm Blakey."

"You have a stand-up basement, Mr. Blakey," the white man told me.

"Say what?"

"Teddy Odett down at Odett Realty said that you had a basement where a man could stand fully erect, one that has electricity and running water."

"This house isn't for sale, mister."

"Bennet. Anniston Bennet. I'm from Greenwich, Connecticut."

"Well this house isn't for sale, Mr. Bennet." I thought the small man would hunch his shoulders, or maybe give me a mean frown if he was used to getting his way. Either way I expected him to leave.

"Oh yes," he said instead. "I know that. Your family has owned this beautiful home for seven generations or more. Mr. Odett told me that. I know it isn't for sale. I'm interested in renting."

"Renting? Like an apartment?"

The man made a face that might have been a smile, or an apology. He let his head loll over his right shoulder and blinked while showing his teeth for a moment.

"Well, not exactly," he said. "I mean yes but not in the conventional way."

His body moved restlessly but his feet stayed planted as if he were a child who was just learning how to speak to adults.

"Well it's not for rent. It's just an old basement. More spiders down there than dust and there's plenty'a dust."

Mr. Bennet's discomfort increased with my refusal. His small hands clenched as if he were holding on to a railing against high winds.

I didn't care. That white man was a fool. We didn't take in white boarders in my part of the Sag Harbor. I was trying to understand why the real-estate agent Teddy Odett would even refer a white man to my neighborhood.

"I want to rent your basement for a couple of months this summer, Mr. Blakey."

"I just told you —"

"I can make it very much worth your while."

It was his tone that cut me off. Suddenly he was one of those no-nonsense-white-men-in-charge. What he seemed to be saying was "I know something that you had better listen to, fool. Here you think you know what's going on when really you don't have a clue."

I knew that there were white people in the Hamptons that rented their homes for four and five thousand dollars a month over the summer. I owned a home like that. It was three stories high and about two hundred years old. It was in excellent shape too. My father had worked at keeping it *up to code*, as he'd say, for most of his life.

"I'm sorry, Mr. Bennet," I said again.

"I'm willing to pay quite a bit for what I want, Mr. Blakey," the white man said, no longer fidgeting or wagging his head. He was looking straight at me with eyes as blue as you please.

"No," I said, a little more certain.

"Maybe this is a bad time. Will you call me when you've had a chance to think about it? Maybe discuss it with your wife?" He handed me a small white business card as he spoke.

"No wife, no roommate, Mr. Bennet. I live alone and I like it like that."

"Sometimes," he said and then hesitated, "sometimes an opportunity can show up just at the right moment. Sometimes that opportunity might be looking you in the face and you don't quite recognize it."

It was almost as if he were threatening me. But he was mild

and unassuming. Maybe it was a sales technique he was working out — that's what I thought at the time.

"Can I call you later to see if you've changed your mind?" he asked.

"You can call all you want," I said, regretting the words as they came out of my mouth. "But I'm not renting anything to anybody."

"Thank you very much for your time, Mr. Blakey." The white man smiled and shook my hand just as if I had said yes to him. "That's my office number in Manhattan on the card. I'd give you my home phone, but I work more than anything else. I hope I'll be hearing from you. If not I will certainly call again."

Before I could say anything else, the little man turned away and walked down to a Volkswagen, the new Bug, parked at the curb. It was a turquoise car that reminded me of an iridescent seven-year beetle.

He made a U-turn and sped away.

Across the street Irene Littleneck was watching from her porch.

"Everything okay, Mr. Blakey?" she called.

"Just a salesman, Miss Littleneck."

"What's he sellin'?"

"I didn't even get to that," I lied. "You don't buy if you're unemployed."

Irene Littleneck, eighty years old and black as tar, flashed her eyes at me. All the way across the road those yellow eyes called me a liar. So I turned my back on them and went into the house.

two

"So you gonna call 'im?" Clarance Mayhew asked me.

"No."

"Why not?" asked Ricky, who was no bigger than one of Clarance's fat legs.

"I don't have an apartment down there, man. I mean there's junk been down there since my mother's mother's mother was a child."

"You could clean it out," Clarance said. His face was chubby and pear shaped. Underneath his chin was a crop of curly hair about an inch thick. Hair wouldn't grow on his cheeks. That's why the tan-colored man always looked about ten years under his actual age. "I mean you ain't got no job so you ain't got no money. You could clean up down there and make yourself somethin' to pay that damn mortgage you took out."

"You want a drink?" I replied.

"Hey." That was Ricky's way of saying yes. He was darker than his cousin but not nearly my color. When my uncle Brent used to see us coming, he'd say, "If it ain't the three shit-colored patches on a tatty brown quilt."

I pulled a bottle of Seagram's from beside the wood chest where we played cards. I took a drink from the bottle and then passed it to Ricky. We never used glasses unless Leonard Butts or Timmy Lee came over to play with us. Clarance, Ricky, and I had drunk from the same bottle since we were babies in the crib.

We were playing blackjack for pennies and I was up $1.25. That meant I had $15.76 left to my name. One more bottle of whiskey and I'd be flat out of money.

"Lemme see some cards," Clarance hissed off the back end of a deep draught of whiskey.

He threw down his three — a heart queen, a deuce, and a trey. Ricky slapped his cards facedown and took the bottle back. I showed two spades, a ten, and an ace.

"Shit," said Clarance. "You got all the luck tonight."

I raked in thirty-seven pennies, thinking about luck and waiting for the bottle.

My aunt Peaches would lend me the money to cover the monthly mortgage payment to the bank. I'd borrowed on the house and Peaches wouldn't let the property slip out of family hands. But if I had to go to her, she'd give me all kinds of grief about how I should get a job and how disappointed my father would have been to see me falling apart like I was.

I took another draught from the bottle. It felt nice. Good whiskey smoothes out after the third sip. Clears the fuzz from behind your eyeballs and relaxes the spine. I've always liked to drink. So did Clarance and Ricky, who we sometimes called Cat.

"Wilson Ryder needs a man to help on those new houses he's putting up," Ricky said.

"Yeah?" I took another drink and realized that I was hoarding the liquor, so I passed it on to Clarance.

"Yeah," Ricky said. "He'll be down there tomorrow. You should go ask 'im."

"Yeah, maybe I will. Maybe so."

"Maybe?" Clarance was shuffling the cards over and over again, the way he always did when he was getting high. "Maybe? Man, what you thinkin'? Like you some kinda prince don't have to work? They will take this house from you, Charles. You gonna end up like old man Bradford—sleepin' in somebody's garage, eatin' day-old bread, and drinkin' brand X."

"Clara, baby," I said, doing my impersonation of a half-hearted lounge lizard. "What's all this tough love, darlin'?"

Clarance had height to carry all that weight. He stood straight up and grabbed for me, but I pushed my chair back and scrambled out of his reach.

"Goddammit, asshole!" he shouted. "I told you not to call me that!"

"But, baby," I pleaded with my hands clasped as if in prayer. "Clara, you tellin' me I ain't worthy."

I knew calling his name in the feminine for the second time would end the card game. We used to tease Clarance in grade school by calling him Clarabell and then just Clara. He stood there shaking, looking as mean as he could manage.

I laughed. And for a moment there was a chance that we would fight. Not much of a chance, because Clarance knew he couldn't take me. But we were both just high enough to act like fools.

Ricky put the bottle down and picked up his sweater. When he stood, that was the signal for Clarance to turn around and leave. Ricky shook his head at me and followed his cousin out the front door.

They'd left their piles of change on the table where we played.

Clarance and I had had these fights for more than twenty-five years. I could still get to him. I regretted it every time. But all Clarance had to do was be himself and he made me mad. He'd always done better than I had. He held a good job as the daytime dispatcher for a colored cab company. He was married, but he still had more girl-friends than I did. He read the newspaper every day and was always referring to events in the world to prove a point when we were discussing politics or current affairs. Even though I had made it through three years of college, Clarance always seemed to know more.

For a while there I had a subscription to the *New York Times* just so I could compete. But I never actually read the paper. Sometimes I'd try to do the crossword puzzle, but that just made me feel stupid. Finally, after losing my job at the bank, I let the subscription go.

I did some things better than Clarance. I was good at sports. But he wouldn't compete with me there. He said I was better than him but I couldn't get a scholarship or anything. And he was right. Like my uncle Brent was always happy to say, "He could win the race, but he cain't beat the clock."

So I tortured Clarance now and then, angry at him for proving my inadequacies.

There were certain benefits to an early evening. The first thing was that there was more than half the fifth of whisky left over. I loved to drink. Loved it. But I didn't abuse alcohol. I never drank before the sun went down and never drove while under the influence. Every once in a while I'd make Ricky and Clarance sleep over when they got too tipsy on a Thursday night.

You'd think I'd want to spend the evening with my friends. As it was I spent almost every night alone, listening to the radio or reading science fiction. I never got into the TV habit. I'd watch the news now and then, but that was mainly to keep up with Clarance. Most nights I spent alone, except when I had a girlfriend. But the last girlfriend I had was Laura Wright. That had ended some months before.

It was mostly just me in the big house. The rooms were large, with big bay windows everywhere. When I was alone I'd wander around in my underwear, talking to myself or reading about outer space. Those were the best moments I had. With the evening spread out in front of me, maybe with some music playing and a few shots of bourbon, I had all the time I needed to think.

I couldn't think when I was around people. In company I was always talking, always telling a joke or laughing at one. My uncle Brent used to say that my mouth was my biggest problem. "Boy," he'd say while sitting in the reclining chair in the den, "if you could just learn to be quiet for a minute, you might hear something worthwhile."

My mother said that I was supposed to love Uncle Brent, but he was hard on children. Brent came to live with us after he had what my mother called *a case of nerves*. There wasn't much wrong with him that I could see, but after his attack he came to live in our house. He kept the garden in the spring and summer and sat in the old chair in what used to be my father's library. But my father was dead by then and Uncle Brent called the library his den.

Brent loved to tell me what was wrong with me. I talked too much, I didn't study enough, I didn't respect authority, and I was way too dark for the genteel colored community of Forest Cove. That was down in South Carolina, where Brent was born. Brent himself was a deep-brown color, with thick lips that were always turned down as if he had a bad taste in his mouth. The only hint he gave of being sick was that it took him a long time to get out of his chair.

So when my mother was out and he'd let loose with one of his insults, I'd say, "Fuck you, old man," and walk slowly away while he struggled to get up and after me. Once outside I'd tear through the backyard and into the family graveyard. From there I'd make it into the ancient stand of sixty-two oaks that my great-great-grandfather Willam P. Dodd planted.

That night in my house, wandering completely naked through the half-dark rooms, I thought about how much fun it was to torture my mean old uncle. When I'd escaped into the dark-green shadows of those gnarly old trees, I'd get the giggles from excitement. Sometimes Brent would stand out on the back porch and yell for me, but he didn't dare to wander off from the house.

He never told my mother about my curses though. I think it was because he was ashamed at not being able to control a child.

The night after the day I met Mr. Anniston Bennet was the first time I'd ever missed Uncle Brent. It had been more than a decade, and I just then marked his passing.

three

I still sleep in my childhood room — in the same bed. The window faces east and the sun streams through every morning, my natural alarm. That Friday I woke up with a headache and a hard-on. I'd been dreaming about Laura, about how she was so excited when I'd carry her up the stairs.

I had to go to the toilet, but I was dizzy. I wanted to jerk off, but my head hurt too much for that. I made myself get up and walk down the second-floor hall to the toilet. It was difficult keeping it in the bowl because the erection was persistent. Even when I finished, it stayed hard.

I went back to bed with the intention of masturbating, but my headache just got worse, and the thought of Laura, as exciting as it was, also made me nauseous.

Finally I got dressed and went downstairs to the kitchen. I wanted coffee, but the percolator was dirty and the sink was full of greasy dishes. There were also dirty dishes piled on the table and sink. I looked at the mess for a while and decided that it was too much for me to do before I had my morning coffee. And so I got my Dodge from the garage and drove down to the Corners for coffee and crumb cake at Hannah and Company.

*

"Morning, Mr. Blakey," Tina Gramble said. She was Hannah's niece, a blond girl with tan skin. She was from a local family and therefore accepted me as part of the community. Being a Negro, I was different. We would never be real friends. But neither of us really wanted that, nor did we feel left out of something. And so it was pleasant when we did cross paths. *Good morning* meant just that.

"Hey, Tina. Could I get some coffee and cake?"

"You look like you could use it," she said, managing to smile and look concerned at the same time.

"Thursday night is blackjack night at my house."

"Hope you won."

"Big."

After my coffee I drove down to the old *highway*, a graded dirt road that led to Canyon's Field. It was the shortcut that would take me most of the way to Wilson Ryder's construction site. The Ryder family had lived in the Harbor for more than 150 years, a long time but not nearly as long as my folks had been around. But you couldn't tell them that. Wilson liked to tell people that his family helped to settle the east end of the island.

Both sides of my family had lived in that area as early as 1742. The Blakeys were indentured servants who earned their freedom. The Dodds were free from the beginning. It was even hinted that they, the Dodds, came straight from Africa at the beginning of the eighteenth century. My parents were both very proud that their ancestors were never slaves. The only time I had ever seen my father get angry was when Clarance's father once asked him, "How can you be sure that one'a them Blakeys you so proud of wasn't a slave at one time or other?"

It was a lovely ride. The woods were deep and green down that way. There were three or four ponds in walking distance from the side of the road. I decided that I'd go fishing after asking Wilson for a job. I planned to tell him that I could begin working that next Monday. That way I could have a long weekend before going back to a job.

A group of eight or nine deer was crossing the road a ways up from me. I came to a stop and so did they. The big female looked at me with hard eyes, trying to glean my intentions. A sigh escaped my throat. I loved to watch deer watching me. They were so timid and ignorant of everything but the possible threat. People think that they're cowardly, but I've been charged by a male or two. I respected them, because with no defense except for their quick feet, they lived out in the wild with no law or protection.

I once saw a group of fifteen or more of them swimming out to Shelter Island. Their heads just above the water, they looked frightened and desperate out there. Cowards don't face terror. Cowards live on back roads, behind closed doors, with the TVs blasting out anything to keep the silence and the darkness from intruding.

The deer's caution made them move slower than they would have without my presence. I enjoyed the show. When the final white tail bobbed off into the wood, I was thoroughly satisfied.

My uncle Brent had been a hunter before he got sick. He killed hundreds of deer down in South Carolina, where he'd lived with his third wife.

"Hunt for the weekend hunters," he'd tell me in one of his few friendly moods. "Kill six bucks and make two forty."

When I was a child I imagined that the deer used to surround our house in the evening, hoping that Brent would come outside for a walk. Then they could stomp him to death for the crimes he'd committed against their race.

*

"Chuck," Wilson Ryder said. The tone of his voice mimicked surprise, but it was also leveled at me offensively.

"Mr. Ryder," I said in greeting. I hated the name Chuck. And he knew it because I had asked him not to call me by that name eighteen years before when I had my first summer job working for his family's construction company.

Wilson Ryder was an older white man with yellowish white hair and a big gut. His family had been in construction for three generations. Young men in my family had worked for his family almost the whole time. He had gray eyes, and fingers covered with yellow-and-black calluses from hard work and cigarettes.

We were standing in a wide circle of yellow soil that had been cleared out of a scrub-pine stand. The trees stood in an angry arc three hundred yards from the center of the circle. There were the beginnings of excavation here and there. Enough to give you the idea of the cul-de-sac of mansions that the Ryder family intended to build. They would level the whole island and sell it off stone by stone if they could.

"What can I do for you?" Ryder asked me.

"I'd like a job, Mr. Ryder."

His gray eyes squinted a hundredth of an inch, maybe less, but it was enough to say that he wasn't going to hire me. Even more than that, the pained wince said that he wouldn't hire me, not because there was no job but because there was something wrong somewhere — something wrong with me.

"You would?" He smiled. There was a yellowy tint to Ryder's teeth too. All that yellow made me feel a little nauseous.

16

"Yes, sir," I said, hating myself for it.

The squint again. This time a little more pronounced.

There were men working on one of the excavations behind the builder, to his right. One man had stopped digging and was looking at me. He was black, I could tell that, but I couldn't make out his features in the distance.

"You worked at that bank, didn't you, Chuck?"

"Charles," I said. "My name is Charles. And yeah, I worked at Harbor Savings."

"Why'd you leave there?"

"Let me go. I don't know. Downsizing, I guess."

Ryder's eyes were very expressive. He was the man in charge and not used to lying. I could see that he was wondering if I believed my own words. That, of course, made me question myself.

"No jobs," he said with a one-shoulder shrug.

I could tell that Ryder wanted me to disappear, just as I had felt about the white man at my door the day before.

But I wasn't going to go away that easily. My family had given Wilson's grandfather one of his first jobs. My grandmother delivered Wilson's brother and sister. He couldn't whisper two words and expect me to go away just like that.

"Well?" he said.

"I thought you had just started hiring."

"It's hard times, Charlie," he said. "You got to get there first if you want to work nowadays."

"But somebody told me last night that you'd still be hiring today."

"Well," Ryder began. He was ready to carry his lie further. But then he looked at me, really I think he was looking at himself, wondering why the hell he was going through all those changes over some unemployed local Negro.

"You used to work for that bank, didn't ya?" he asked.

"Yeah?"

"Why aren't you there anymore?"

"I don't know. They just let me go."

"Well let's just say that I'm lettin' you go too."

It didn't make any sense. How could he let me go if I didn't even work for him? I almost said something about it, but I knew that I'd just sound stupid.

Wilson gave me a crooked little smile and friendly nod. *Can't win 'em all* — that's what the gesture meant.

I cursed him all the way down the road to the town of Sag Harbor.

I grabbed a clam roll and a beer at the stand down by the pier, using the last of my paper dollars to pay for the meal. From then on I'd have to pay for whatever I bought in change. I could already hear the teenage cashiers snickering behind my back.

If suicide meant just giving up, I would have dropped dead at that moment. With no job, no money, and no chance for a job, I was as close to penniless as a man can get.

"Negro so poor," my uncle Brent used to say of his less-fortunate brothers, "that he'd sell his shadow just to stand in your shade."

The weather was pleasant. I went to the end of the pier and looked down at the tiny fishes coming up to get warm in the weak sunlight. Two small jellyfish were waving in the current. I sat on the edge of the big concrete dock and stared down at the water. That was 10:45. At 12:15 I was still there. From the time I was a child, I'd have moments like that. In class if I saw something interesting, usually something natural, I could stare the whole period long. I never thought anything at these times. I just stared at the spiderweb or the furious bird making her nest. One time I watched an ant search the entire third-grade floor for nearly an hour. She finally ended up under Mrs. Harkness's shoe. I was so shocked by the sudden death that I broke down crying and was sent to the nurse.

I hadn't been in the bank since I was laid off nine months before. Arnold Mathias was still at his post by the door. Less a guard than a greeter, he knew everybody's name and any special need that he or she might have.

"Hello, Millie," he said to the octogenarian Mildred Cosgrove, who doddered in before me. "Mr. Hickey isn't in today. He's got flu, I believe."

"Oh," the old lady said. There was shock and pain in her voice. While she stood there, Arnold looked over her head and saw me. He put up a hand, not in greeting but to stop me until he had finished with Millie Cosgrove.

"Will he be in later?" she asked in a fearful, tremulous voice.

"He won't be back until next week, Millie." Mathias, himself in his late sixties and shaky, held out a hand to steady the older woman.

"Oh," she said again. "Well maybe I better wait until Monday then. You know Mr. Hickey has all my records. He knows what I want. Monday you say?"

"I'm sure he'll be back by then," Mathias said. "And if he comes back earlier, I'll have him call you."

"That would be nice. Yes. You know I have to take my money out of the stock market before the world goes to hell in a handbasket. He talked me into it before, but now I just want a passbook. I want regular interest with no nonsense.

The stock market is no better than roulette, and gambling is a sin."

"I'm sure Mr. Hickey will do what you want..."

The conversation went on for another few minutes. Mr. Mathias listened to Mildred's woes. Everyone knew that old Mrs. Cosgrove had barely a hundred-dollar balance in her account. She lived off social-security checks. But her family had been some of the bank's first depositors. Treating her nicely was the best advertisement they could have.

"Yes, Charles?" the guard asked after Millie left. "Can I help you?"

"No."

"Did you want something?"

"Can't anyone walk into this bank, Arnold?"

"Of course. But I didn't think that you had an account here anymore."

"I came to see Lainie," I said.

"Oh, I see. Lainie."

The greeter had reverted into guard and had no intention of standing aside. So I went around him and across the wide tiled floor of the bank.

It was a domed building with a round floor. At the opposite side from the entrance was a group of seven desks, separated from the main room by a waist-high mahogany wall. The center desk belonged to Lainie Brown.

Lainie was the only black bank officer. She'd started as secretary the year I was born. Her boss was a liberal thinker, and she trained Lainie and then forced the bank president, Ira Minder, to promote her.

Lainie had been my friend at the bank. We ate lunch together, and she told me that she hoped to make me into a loan officer one day. But then I was fired, and that was the end to my banking future and our friendship.

"Charles." Lainie was surprised but not necessarily happy to see me. She was a heavyset woman with auburn skin. Her eyes were large and spaced wider than most. Every tooth had a space between it, and her smile, when she smiled, seemed to wrap around her whole head.

But Lainie wasn't smiling right then. Her look was somewhere between surprise and caution. I might have been a snake on her front porch or a strange purple sky.

"'Bout time for lunch, isn't it?" I said.

"Uh, why I suppose it is."

"I already ate, but I'll sit with you if you don't mind."

"No," her lips said. Her eyes held the same answer with another meaning. I suppose somebody else might have taken the hint and offered to wait until a better time.

"Well, let's go," I said.

Lainie rose up out of her generous walnut seat, releasing a sweet odor. Her perfume was one of the best benefits at Harbor Savings. It was one of the few things I remembered about work.

four

Lainie ate a bagged lunch every day at 12:30. Ham or turkey or chicken on white bread, with a fruit and a novelty cake. She sat on the picnic bench half a block up from the Winter Hotel on a slip of property that was too small to sell. She was wearing a white silk dress that was decorated with prints of giant purple orchids. A single pearl hung from a pendant around her neck. There was a dark freckle on her throat, next to the pearl. I was thinking that that small spot of dark flesh was far more precious than some stone from an oyster's belly.

"How's Peaches?" Lainie had regained her composure. She'd opened her bag and was peeling back the wax paper on the sandwich to check out the meat.

"Fine, the last time I talked to her. Her husband's mother passed."

"I know. I was at the funeral. I was surprised not to see you there."

"Busy," I said, not remembering the excuse I gave at the time.

Lainie took a bite out of her sandwich and smiled. She always smiled after the first bite of her sandwich. She told me once that her mother, Arvette, made her lunch every morning.

I think the bread reminded Lainie of her mother the way that Catholics are supposed to be reminded of their Lord when they eat that biscuit.

Lainie and Arvette lived together just outside of town in a small house where both of them had been born. Most Negroes around the mid-island lived in modest homes. Our ancestors had been farmworkers mainly. Many had come from the South over the decades, looking for a place they could work in peace.

"I was out at Wilson Ryder's new site this morning," I said.

"Really? Mr. Gurgel is the officer in charge of that loan. He says that the Ryders have always been good business." She took another bite. But that was just eating — no smile involved.

"Yeah. Well, anyway, I went over there to ask about a job today. I mean, he had jobs. I know that because Ricky Winkler works out there. But Mr. Ryder lied and said that he didn't have any jobs. And when I told him that he was a liar, he started talkin' about the bank and why didn't I work there anymore?"

Lainie took a big bite out of her sandwich. I think she did that because she wanted time to think. After chewing on her white bread and processed meat like it was a mouthful of jerky, she stopped and took a deep breath. I pushed down the urge to stand up and walk away.

"Did you ever take money from your drawer?" she asked.

And suddenly it all came back to me like the plot of a novel that I had read so long ago I didn't even remember the name of the book. But it wasn't that long ago and it was my own life that I was remembering.

It wasn't really very much at all. I was a bank teller. I counted money, gave change, made debits and credits. I did

passbooks, Christmas clubs, checking accounts, and sometimes payroll. Anything else went to another window. I wore
a jacket and slacks every day with a tie. You didn't have to
wear the tie on Fridays, but I did anyway. I was good at my
job. Always on time, friendly with even the rude customers, I
was good at math too.

But one day I was going to meet my then-girlfriend China
Browne for dinner. It was a Tuesday and I wasn't due for my
paycheck until the end of the week. My account was empty
because I had just paid for an electric food processor and
China wanted to be taken out.

So I borrowed twenty dollars from the bank. I made up my
mind to pay a dollar interest when I got my paycheck. And it
really wasn't any big sum. If they asked me about it, I could
just say that I must have made a mistake. People make
mistakes in banks all the time. Mr. Gurgel, the senior loan
officer, once missed a zero and the bank was out ninety
thousand dollars for a week.

Of course Friday came and went. China and I went down
to New York that weekend, so I put off returning the
twenty until I got paid again. But by that time two more
weeks had passed, and I figured if nobody noticed, then
why should I worry? Probably if I had left it at that, everything would have been okay. But there were five or six other
times when I needed money. It was never more than fifty
dollars.

"No," I said.

"Well that's what they thought," she said. "The president
said that they had proof."

"How could that be?" I felt indignant even though I knew
that I was guilty. "If they had proof, then why didn't they
have me arrested?"

"Mr. Mathias told me that they had discussed it and the bank felt it wouldn't serve their interests to prosecute." I knew that she was reporting what she heard because the words she was using were not hers.

"Why not?"

"Because it wasn't a lot of money and almost every colored person in the Harbor has money in the bank. If the bank prosecuted you over a couple'a hundred dollars, the customers might get upset and take their money to East Hampton." Lainie peered into my eyes as she spoke. I don't know if she saw my guilt there or not.

I was guilty. Every time I pocketed a few dollars, I expected to return it. But it wasn't like the money I used to steal out of my uncle Brent's wallet. I took that money because I hated him. I hated the way he smelled and the way he talked about my father. I took it because my father's family had come directly from Africa, but Brent said that my father really didn't know our roots. He said that we were like all other American blacks, that we came from "slave-caliber Negroes who were defeated in war and sold into slavery because they didn't have the guts to die in battle." He said that there was no such thing as free Africans who had "chosen to come over and sell their labor in indentured servitude" and that American Negro citizens never existed before 1865, as my father claimed.

I kept Brent's money. He used to complain to my mother, but I'd just tell her that it must be his illness affecting his brain. I don't know what she thought about it all. She didn't like Brent's mouth either, but he was family and my mother was the sweetest woman in the world.

"Well," I said to Lainie. "I didn't steal anything and now people at the bank are telling everybody that I'm a thief and

I can't get a job. And you didn't even tell me. Didn't warn me or anything."

"I'm sorry, Charles," she said. "I just didn't know what to think. Mr. Mathias told me about what had happened. And I was afraid that you'd lose your temper and that if they did have some kind of evidence that they'd take you to jail. I was worried about you."

She was getting weepy. Lainie had a kind heart. But I wasn't in any mood to worry about her crocodile tears. What about me? Here I had waited until I was down to my last dollar, thinking that I could always pick up a job somewhere. But nobody in the Harbor would hire a thief. And even if I went out of town, people would still ask for references.

What I wanted to do was yell at Lainie until she felt the pain that I was feeling on the inside. I would have yelled if I were innocent.

"I'm sorry, Lainie. It's not your fault. It's just that bank. I probably made some mistake and they decided that I was a thief. That's all."

"What are you going to do?"

I considered her question for a moment, and then I thought a little more. I opened my mouth, but there was no answer forthcoming.

"I got to go," I said. "Thanks for tellin' me."

five

I did go fishing — in a small river not two miles from my house. I caught three good-size trout, not for pleasure but to eat that night. I wanted to cook dinner but couldn't bear the idea of counting out pennies to some high school cashier at the IGA.

It was after 6:00 when I got home. There was a little daylight left in the distance, but it was dusk. My plans were all set by the time I got in, so I went right to the phone.

A woman answered after seven rings. "Hello?"

"Mona?"

"Hey, Charles. Hold on." She put the phone down with a loud knock and yelled, "It's Charles!"

A few moments passed and then the phone hissed as it was being picked up.

"What?" a man's angry voice said.

"Hey, Clarance. Listen, man, I got to borrow a hundred bucks fast."

"So?"

"This is no joke, Clarance —"

"Naw. That's right. This ain't no joke at all. This is dead

27

serious. I been thinkin' about you and how you act since last night. And it burns me up. Here I am tryin' to be your friend and all you wanna do is dis me. Well that's it. I'm through with you, man. I called Ricky and told him. I said no more Thursday-night blackjack, no more Saturday-night bar hoppin', no more nuthin'. We're through." Clarence was sputtering. I almost made a joke but then thought better of it.

"Hey," I said. "I'm sorry. I didn't mean nuthin'. You know it was the whiskey —"

"You sorry all right. Unemployed, drunk loudmouth is what you is." Clarence usually tried to articulate in the ways of school learning. That kind of language was promoted among the older colored families of the Harbor. But when he got angry, he talked *street*.

"I said I was sorry, man. What more do you want?"

"I don't want nuthin' from you. I don't want you to call or ask me for money or nuthin' else. Just stay away from me, you hear?" And with that he hung up the phone in my ear.

I realized then that I didn't have any kind of plan. All I was going to do was borrow a hundred dollars from Clarence to put some cheap food in my refrigerator.

I washed out a griddle and a saucepan, a glass and a plate and utensils to cook and eat with. Then I cleaned my fish and dredged the fillets in cornmeal. Fried fish with hot sauce and a side of turnips was my dinner. I laughed because it was better food than I would have had if I had the money to go to the diner.

There were two shots' worth left in the whiskey bottle, just enough to keep me between self-pity and drunken tears.

The house was a mess. There were piles of clothes and dirty dishes in every room. Junk mail and bills were thrown into corners, and every chair had something piled on the seat.

I went upstairs to my bedroom and threw the blankets —
along with a notebook, two dirty dinner plates, and a dozen
loose stones that I had picked up — from the bed. I lay with
arms and legs dangling over the sides of the small mattress.
On the windowsill next to my head was a book I had been
reading. *Neglect's Glasses*. It was a science-fiction novel
about a kid in the ghetto who had found a pair of sunglasses
somehow imbued with the intelligence of an alien race. The
ghetto child, just days away from his initiation into a youth
gang, is drawn into a swirl of knowledge that takes him
places that he never knew were possible.

I laid there on my bed, reading, for well over an hour. The
boy, whose name was Tyler, was transformed into the
unknown hope of humanity. He did good things because the
glasses always made him feel the emotions of those lives he
touched. And so when he hurt people, he experienced their
pain. Helping others made Tyler feel good about himself.

I would have read the whole book that night if it wasn't for
chapter twelve. That's where Tyler looked closely at his
parents and in a flash of divination realized that his father
would soon be dead. I couldn't take the revelation and threw
the slender hardback into the tin trash can, decorated with
astronauts, that had sat in the same corner for more than
thirty years. The book hitting the can set off a burble of beer
bottles jostling together.

There were five empties in the can under a holey T-shirt
and a few wads of paper. I found four more under the bed.
On the outside of the windowsill, there was one dead soldier,
as Clarance called them. That started my journey back
through the house. There were bottles everywhere. Some
were only half empty. One or two almost full. There were
bottles on the front porch, in the backyard, on the patio

chairs. On the roof there were a few left over from friendly spring nights when Laura and I made love in my sleeping bag up under the stars.

They were behind the couch and on the inside ledge of the fireplace. By the time I finished, there were fifty-one bottles on the old dining-room table. Those empties would make me two paper dollars. And with them I could keep my pride.

I remembered what I was doing and who I was with for almost every bottle found. The ones in the backyard were from a party the summer before last. It was Ricky and Clarance with some other guys and girls. The police had to come over to tell us to turn the music down.

It was the only time in my life that I had sex with two women in one night. The first was my girlfriend at that time, China Browne. We'd been dancing and got to get kind of amorous. I took her up to my mother's old room. It was over pretty quickly because I was so excited. China fell asleep and I went back downstairs. There were lots of people there dancing and talking loud. I felt a sweet sense of calm and started putting beer bottles back in a wooden crate. China's friend Jane Sadler started picking up with me.

We were just talking and laughing about what a good time everybody was having. We filled two crates and were carrying them out to the backyard. Then we heard this noise, a moaning out behind the garage. I winked at Jane and we snuck around the corner.

It was Clarance and this white girl who had come with somebody, I didn't know who. But she was with Clarance right then. They were kissing furiously in the faint light that shone over the back of the garage. He was moaning in a deep bass and she squealed between their soul kisses.

Jane put her hand on my forearm. At first I thought that

she wanted to give the newfound lovers some privacy, but when I looked I could see that she was just steadying herself. Jane had skin my color and bright eyes and long curly hair.

Suddenly Clarance spun the white girl around. She lifted her miniskirt while he pulled down her panties. Jane's grip on my forearm tightened. Clarance started fumbling with his zipper then. The white girl was waving her butt around and moaning. Clarance kept fumbling.

"Hurry up!" The white girl's hushed cry was exactly what I wanted to shout.

"I got it now," Clarance said, throwing down something. The next morning I realized that it was the wrapper from a condom.

He bent his knees and took a long slow slide into his new friend. Her welcoming moan made my heart skip so hard that I thought I might be having a seizure.

Clarance started slamming hard against her backside. The smacking flesh and high-pitched barks from the girl made me sweat.

"I cain't hold it, baby," Clarance barked. "I cain't hold it."

"Come come come come come," she answered.

And then they were both silent and rigid. After a moment Clarance made a grunting sound that was no more than the crack of a dry leaf and the girl exhaled through her open mouth.

Jane pulled me by the arm. When we got around to the other side, she kissed me. I led her straight to the basement.

There was no inside connection from the house. You had to go outside and through a heavy trapdoor to get down there. I suppose that it was called a basement because it was under the house, but it was more like a crypt.

I snapped on the light and Jane kissed me again.

"Don't say a word," she told me as she lifted her skirt and I dropped my pants. She sat back on my great-grandfather's oversize traveling trunk.

It should have been safe sex but it wasn't. I was happy that I just made love to China because I didn't want those moments with Jane to ever end. I rocked back and forth on the balls of my feet while she stroked my other balls and scratched both of my nipples with the long, press-on fingernails of one hand. We were looking into each other's eyes. Every once in a while she'd lean forward to kiss me, but when I returned the gesture she moved her head back and sneered.

The trunk rocked precariously, but we had the balance of cats in heat. She undulated on her hips and quivered while I pushed and pulled, feeling the veins standing out all over my body. I started to move faster but Jane said, "Slow it down, baby. Slow it down."

When I finally came I moved back in one small show of responsibility. The emotion on her face while she watched my ejaculation was the deep satisfaction that comes from victory.

China stopped seeing me after that night, and Jane never returned one phone call. Maybe they compared notes; I didn't care. That night was a highlight for me. Two women and a chance to see the Master — that's what we called Clarance when it came to women — in action. I was at peace for a whole week. I didn't do anything except pack the trash into bags and put the crates of empty beers in the basement.

That's why I thought about the basement. It was Jane and China Browne that jarred my memory.

It was a large, dark room crowded with stuff from the Dodd and Blakey families. A little something was there from every generation. I had one great-auntie, Blythe, who considered herself a painter. There were fifty or more of her awful canvases leaned up against the walls and behind a useless coal-burning stove. Her trees and houses and people looked like a child's pitiful attempts. There was my great-grand-father's traveling trunk and stacks of old newspapers that were yellow and brittle from fifty years or more before. We had old furniture and rugs and straw baskets filled with two hundred Christmases of toys. The cobwebs looked like they belonged on a movie set, and it was cold down there too.

Eighteen wooden crates of empty beer bottles were stacked in the middle of the cobblestone floor. They were all I was interested in. It meant twenty-four dollars at the beer-and-soda store at the Corners. I dragged the boxes out into the light, rubbing my face now and then to get off the tickle of cobwebs. When I got all the crates, I looked around some more to see if there might have been something else of value there.

It *was* a big basement. Thirty feet in either direction. The ceiling must have been ten feet from the floor. Anniston Bennet was right: it would have made a nice apartment without all that junk. It was a well-built hole. Dry as a bone and cool year round because it was deep in the rocky earth. I used to think that ghosts lived in that cellar, that the spirits of my dead ancestors came from out of the graveyard behind my house and played cards or talked all night long in the solitude of that room. I left them Kool-Aid and lemon cookies in the summer. When the food was still there the next day, my father would tell me that the spirits had eaten the ghost food that lives inside the food for the living. He told me that it was like a blessing and now the food left over had to be buried in the trash like the dead.

six

Late the next day I was in my newly cleaned kitchen, ready to cook.

Twenty-four dollars can buy a lot of canned spinach and baked beans. I also got rice and polenta and a big bag of potatoes. One whole chicken with celery and carrots could make a soup to last me a week if I stretched it.

I'm not a good cook, but I can make simple dishes. That's because I used to love spending time with my mother in the kitchen. She never made me work. All I had to do was sit around and make her laugh. That was until eighth grade. Then, when she got sick, I helped out a lot. Brent said that my mother had to work through it, that being sick was all in her head. He was healthier than she was and still expected to get waited on.

My chicken was boiling and I was cutting celery into slantwise strips and suddenly it came to me. I dug Anniston Bennet's card out of my pocket and dialed his Manhattan number. It wasn't until the fourth ring that I remembered it was Saturday. I thought that at least I could leave a message. He didn't give me a home phone anyway. His name, in lower case blue letters, was centered on the white card, and the phone number was in the lower right-hand corner in red.

"Hello," a woman's voice said. I almost answered but the surprisingly natural-sounding recording continued, "You have reached the Tanenbaum and Ross Investment Strategies Group." Then there was a click and the same woman, in a different mood, said, "Mr. Bennet," then another click and she was back on track saying, "is not in at the moment but will return your message at the earliest possible time. Please leave your name and number after the signal." Then there came a complex set of tones that sounded something like a police siren in a foreign film.

"Mr. Bennet? This is Charles Blakey from out in the Harbor. I guess I'd like to talk to you about what it is you want exactly. I mean, maybe uh, maybe we can come to some kind of arrangement. I don't know. My number is..." Leaving information on an answering machine always seems useless to me. Most of the messages I've left have gone unanswered. I didn't have much hope that anything would work out. Anyway it was early May and all I had was a pocketful of change. A summer rental wasn't going to do much for me right then.

So I called my aunt Peaches. That was her real name. Her mother was Clementine and her father was actually named Apollodorus. My father used to say, when we were going to Clemmie's for Thanksgiving dinner, "Well let's go over and visit the mouthful."

"Hi, Aunt Peaches. It's me — Charles."

"Yes, Charles?" She wasn't sounding generous.

"How's your family?"

"Everybody's fine."

"That's good," I said and then waited for her to ask after my health.

She did not.

"It's been a while since I've seen you, Peaches."

"Has it?"

She knew full well that it had been more than three years since I had been by, and I was only allowed in then because her husband was at work. We didn't live more than two miles apart, but the only time I ever saw her was if we happened to bump into each other in town. That was because of her husband, Floyd. Floyd Richardson was a lawyer who practiced in Long Island City. When I dropped out of college, he hired me — *to make something out of me*, he said.

Well, I was only twenty-one and not really ready to work that hard. I didn't like the law or research. I wanted to be a sailor. Floyd and I had a rough time of it. When he finally fired me, he told me that I was a shame to my race. That reminded me of Uncle Brent, who always added, "The human race."

After that I wasn't a welcomed guest in their home. Floyd rarely gave me a nod if we passed in the street. I didn't mind much. Floyd wanted to act like he was my father, like it was him who did for me. Aunt Peaches was nice, but she was so formal that talking to her was like being read to from a book of etiquette.

"I needed to ask you something," I said, having given up any hope that we could be friendly.

"I really don't have much time, Charles. Floyd's coming home soon and I have to get his dinner."

"Well, you know I lost my job," I started.

"Oh?"

"I had some money left over from that T-bill Mom left for me when I turned thirty, but that's all gone." I paused but Peaches had no consolations to give. "And, well, I kind of borrowed some money on the house. I'm looking for work, but I still have to come up with the payment. It's already two weeks overdue."

Peaches didn't say a word, but the quality of her silence had changed. I could almost feel her growing anxiety.

"Peaches?"

"Why do you want to do this to me, Charles?"

"What am I doing to you?"

"You're thirty-nine years old —"

"Thirty-three," I corrected.

"— thirty-three years old and you don't even have two nickels to rub together. What would your mother say?"

"My mother is dead. Maybe you could leave her alone."

"Rude." She said the word like it was a club to bludgeon me with. "Rude. And then you want me to write the check. I'm sorry, Charles, but I have to agree with Floyd about you. There's no helping someone who can't help himself. I just hope you don't lose our family home with your foolishness. But maybe it would be better in someone else's hands anyway. I can see you don't have a gardener anymore and from what I hear it's a pigsty on the inside."

I hung up. It was the only way I could get her to feel the pain that she was inflicting on me. I knew she was right. I knew that my life was messed up. But what could I do about it when I couldn't get a job or pay my bills?

I spent the entire night cleaning. I collected eight big plastic bags of trash. I swept and dusted and mopped and straightened. When I'd get tired I'd stop for a little chicken soup and black tea. Then I was off again, up and down through the three floors. At 4:00 in the morning I dragged the bags out of the house and into the street. I wasn't going to let Peaches and Floyd defeat me. I'd put the house in perfect shape. I had plans to wax the floors and mow the lawn. I'd trim the hedge too. After that I'd paint the house. This last thought almost defeated me. How could I paint with no money? I couldn't even buy a roller or brush, much less all the gallons of paint that I'd need.

Outside I noticed a spark. At first I thought it was a firefly, and I stopped to catch a glimpse of it again. Fireflies were a miracle to me. The fact of their light seemed somehow to prove that there was a God.

After a moment the light appeared again. But it wasn't a firefly at all. It was Miss Littleneck smoking a cigarette in the dark. At first I was mad, thinking that she was spying on me. But then I thought that if she was really spying, she wouldn't be advertising with an ember. It was almost as amazing as a firefly — that old woman sitting out on her porch all night long, smoking one cigarette after another, waiting for either a miracle or a heart attack.

The next day was Sunday. I'd fallen asleep on the sofa in my father's library. After three hours' sleep I was out in the front yard with a scythe.

That was a gas.

Christ's Hope Church was just three blocks up from my house and many a churchgoer had to drive past my place. Almost everyone slowed to see me stripped to the waist, cutting down the dead weeds and grasses that had grown wild for years.

Peaches and Floyd drove by. They came to a virtual stop in order to gawk. I smiled at them and waved. Peaches said something to her husband and they sped off to God.

seven

That was one of the hardest days I ever put in. Twelve thirty-nine-gallon plastic bags of trash and dead weeds. I only had two empty bags left. In the afternoon I broke my fast with instant coffee, baked beans, and quick-cooking polenta. I carried the meal on a tray up to the third floor, to my mother's sewing room, which was a small chamber off her bedroom. There she had a treadle-powered sewing machine and a small table meant for piecework.

I put my tray on the table and stared out the window like I used to do as a child when my parents were out. Her window was the observation deck for my fortress. I could see our family graveyard and my great-grandfather's stand of oaks and then up the side of the piney hills behind our community. As a child I sat there for hours shooting BBs at Confederate soldiers or the English. I was a patriotic Yankee fighting to protect my home.

My mother was still alive in that room. The basket with her threads and yarns sat next to her spindly maple chair. Her worn sewing slippers lay underneath the table, making it seem as if she would soon be coming up to use them. I could see her in my mind, long face and coffee-and-cream-colored skin. Her nose was broad but not so flat and her eyes were as round as some forest creature's orbs. She always smiled just to see me. That smile was always waiting for me upstairs in her room.

My father was dimmer in my memory. Much darker than Mom, he was thick. Not fat but strong like a tree trunk. He had big hands and a giant's laugh. Nobody expected him to drop dead, certainly not me. Maybe if I had warning I would have looked closer, listened more attentively while he was still alive. As it is he's just a big hole in my memory, a hole where there was a yearning. I looked away over the hills because if I paid too much attention to my father's absence, the yearning would turn into a yowl.

A dead leaf from the previous fall was tumbling on a sudden wind. Its progress was almost musical; it seemed to be tinkling in the breeze. I looked and listened and then realized that the phone was ringing downstairs.

My foot hit the last step to the first floor when the ringing stopped. The leaf was still blowing in my mind's eye and I was laughing. I sat down next to the phone, wondering whether or not to go up for my beans and cornmeal. My hesitation was rewarded with another ring.

There was a great deal of static over the line.

"Hello."

"Mr. Blakey. Anniston Bennet."

"Oh, Mr. Bennet. I didn't expect to hear from you until at least tomorrow."

"I call into my messages every six hours unless I'm somewhere where I can't get to a phone. You're interested in renting me your basement?"

"We can talk about it."

I thought I heard the hiss of a sharp intake of breath.

Maybe it was the bad connection, but I got the feeling that Mr. Bennet was not a patient man.

"I don't have time to come out there again, Mr. Blakey."

"Well, I don't know what to tell you then."

We were silent for a few beats while the chatter of the static went merrily along. At one point I thought the connection might have broken off.

"I can come out there on Friday," Bennet said in a restrained tone. Another conversation interfered with us over the lines. It was some foreign tongue, sounded Arabic but I'm not too good with languages.

"What time?" I asked over the new conversation.

"Four. Four in the afternoon."

"I'll see you at four then."

"Four," Anniston Bennet said one more time, and the connection was broken.

There I sat, listening to phone static from some foreign land, happy even though I had just made the first step toward giving up my solitude. I tried to imagine the little white man coming into my kitchen while I was standing there in my drawers with a hangover.

From there I wondered about the word *hangover* for a while. Was it an old seafaring term? Was the image of a sailor throwing up over the side of the ship, hanging on for his life? That brought me around to thinking about liquor, Southern Comfort to be exact. Ricky loved Southern Comfort and I did too.

"Hey, Cat," I said into the receiver.

"Charles, hey."

"You doin' anything?"

"Uh-uh, man. Not me. Clarance out with his wife an' kids. He sure don't wanna see you after Thursday night."

"Yeah." I paused, anticipating the drink. "Hey, Ricky?"

"Hey what?"

"You wanna pick up a pint of SC and come on over?"

"Shit."

"I'll pay you for the whole thing when you get here, man." That was a good offer and Ricky knew it. "I need some help with my basement."

"Okay," he said. "I gotta give my sister a ride, but then I'll be over."

"Is it dry?" Ricky asked, holding his tumbler of iced Southern Comfort and peering down into the darkness of the cellar.

"Yeah. These doors are triple ply and high. No rain can get in." I took a few steps down and pulled the chain on the light.

Ricky followed.

"Big down here," he said.

"All this junk, man. I gotta get rid of it."

"Why? You gonna rent to that white man?"

"No," I lied.

I've lied all my life. To my parents and teachers and friends at school. I lied about being sick and not coming in to work, about romantic conquests, my salary, my father's job. I've lied about where I was last night and where I was right then if I was on the phone and no one could see me. I have lied and been called a liar and then lied again to cover other falsehoods. Sometimes I pretend to know things that I don't know. Sometimes I lie to tell people what I think they want to hear.

It's not such a bad thing — lying. Sometimes it protects people's feelings or gives them confidence or just makes them laugh.

But I never told a lie like that one-word fib to Ricky about Anniston Bennet. Somehow I knew that I shouldn't talk about the little man who calls from Arabia about a basement sublet. I wanted to keep those cards close to my vest.

"Damn, you got some old stuff down here," Ricky was saying.

"Junk."

"Uh-uh, man. This is antique-quality shit."

"Shit is right."

"No, Charles. These old dolls and wood toys are valuable. So's the furniture, the trunk, probably the clothes in the trunk, and maybe even these old paintings. You can't tell, man. These people out here spend five hundred dollars on an old broked-down chair in a minute." Ricky had lived his teenage years in Brooklyn with his father. The way he talked was different than the way most of my friends did. But he had an eye for profit. One summer he and Clarance ran a nighttime hot-dog stand in East Hampton. Charged three and four dollars for hot dogs, and got it.

"How do I sell this stuff? Yard sale?"

"That's sucker shit right there, man. Uh-uh. There's some dealers in East Hampton and Southampton. I know who they are, but you know they wanna rob you. But there's this sister out around Bridgehampton run a little store that specializes in old quilts. Narciss Gully. If we could get Narciss out here to look at your stuff and then broker it with the other dealers, then you might make out."

"You know her?"

"Ten percent."

"Say what?" My tumbler was empty and I just felt the Southern Comfort in my blood.

"Ten percent," Ricky said again. "I don't do any manual labor and I'm not responsible if at the end you don't think you got enough money."

"What does she get out of it?"

"I'll suggest ten percent for her too, but she might ask for as much as twenty."

"Thirty percent gone and you two don't do nothing but introduce?" I was arguing, but I knew it was a lost cause. I had the woman's name; I could have called her on my own. But that would have cut Ricky out — I would never have treated a friend like that.

I spent the next day pulling junk out of my basement. It was a day full of the dry husks of spiders and centipedes, and dust on top of oily grime that had been laid down before the Civil War. I washed and swept and scrubbed with every brush I had — even my uncle Brent's old toothbrush. My work yielded six boxes of old books (including three diaries from three generations of Blakeys and Dodds), wooden toys, tools that I couldn't even figure out how to hold, and so many piles of old clothes that I could only make a stab at separating them. Tuxedos and jeans, fancy dresses and all kinds of undergarment straps, dried-up elastics, and buckles. Most of the clothes looked like they could have been for children, but it was just that I had a long line of short people in my family. My parents were only the second generation of big Blakeys. I'm six foot two. My father was six one.

I moved all the furniture out of the living room and brought in the loot, piling it in each of the corners according to type. When the job was done, I sat in the wide seat of the bay window to appreciate my labor.

I liked hard work. A big pile of stones that need to be moved, a field to plow. What I love is a big job that takes muscle and stick-to-itiveness. I'm not into a lot of details or measuring or comparing. I don't want to build a steam engine; just give me a sledgehammer or a shovel and I can work all day long, all month if I have to.

"Hello?" The voice came from the front door, which was open. "Mr. Blakey?"

I had been asleep. The room around me was dim because there was no light on and the sun was setting outside.

"Mr. Blakey?" She was tall and thin, brittle looking on first glance. That was probably because she was so tentative coming into a stranger's home.

"Over here," I said. My voice was heavy from sleep, but there was a quality to it that was different. I don't know if you want to call it musical or assured or maybe mature, like a man.

"Charles Blakey?" the tall woman asked.

"Yeah. And I guess you're Narciss Gully."

Hearing her name calmed the skittish woman a bit.

"Oh," she said. "It was dark and I didn't know..."

I went to the wall near where she'd entered the room and turned on the light.

"...didn't know if something was wrong." She was brown, mostly dark brown, but here and there it lightened a little, lending a subtle texture to her skin. I imagined the broad sweep of clouds across the earth from an astronaut's view. Or maybe it was a parchment, incredibly old and almost erased by age and rain, the slight gradation of color coming from sepia glyphs whose secrets were now gone.

"...I mean it was so dark," she continued, obviously still nervous about coming into a strange man's house without the proper reception.

I didn't help to relieve her fears, looking her over, thinking strange thoughts about her skin.

"...and you were just sitting there..."

"I've been working all day pulling stuff out of the cellar because Ricky said you'd come by at eight. I guess I worked so hard that I fell asleep here in the window." And there it was — the truth. There was no lie in my words, body language, or voice. And again I wondered what had happened. It was almost as if I were in one of my beloved Philip José Farmer fantasies. Like I had gone to sleep in a mundane world and awakened in a fantastical place where the colors were brighter and youth was eternal. It was partially like that, like some fantasy, but this new world of mine was only subtly different; only my point of view and clarity of vision had altered.

"Oh," Narciss said, looking around the large living room. "There's a lot, isn't there?"

She wasn't a beautiful woman, except for that skin. Probably my age, give or take. Her face was squarish and the white-rimmed glasses were too big for her features. Her eyes were a muddy color and her fingers were too long it seemed. But when she splayed out those digits to indicate the immensity of the trove I had uncovered, I appreciated their reach.

"You think it's worth anything?"

"I can't tell until I've studied it, but it certainly looks interesting."

"Hey, Charles?" came another voice.

"In here, Ricky," I said.

When he came in I was disappointed because he wasn't carrying a bottle in a bag. Whenever I heard Ricky's voice, I got the urge to drink. I wondered then how often since we were children that we had been sober together.

"Hey, Narciss. How are you?"

"Fine, Richard," she said.

"You guys met, huh?"

"Yeah, Cat." Ricky winced when I called him by his nickname. I didn't use it again that night.

Narciss was already down on her knees, looking through the toys. She had on close-fitting khaki trousers with a matching woman's jacket. She took off the jacket, revealing a loose black T-shirt. She was dressed for hard work.

While she worked Ricky and I sat side by side in the window seat, watching her plow through my family's accumulation of junk.

"You wanna go get a shot at Bernie's?" Ricky asked me.

That meant the drinks were on him. That was our code — the man who suggested drinks paid for them.

I wanted to go. But I was also interested in everything about Narciss. By then she was sitting in a half-lotus position, going over old photographs and letters that my mother kept in a miniature steamer trunk she'd inherited from some aunt or another. With every new letter she clucked her tongue or hummed. I felt like she was a teacher impressed by my homework assignment.

Narciss was marking out a history that would probably have captured the interest of historians and anthropologists around the nation. But for me there was only her, scrutinizing a pile of refuse that, if it weren't for her concern, I would have used to make a bonfire in the backyard.

eight

Ricky was fidgety. He wasn't used to sitting around while others worked.

"I saw Clarance last night," he said.

"What's he have to say?"

"Nuthin'. He's gonna add a rumpus room onto the house this summer. He asked if I could work on it, but I told him that I was already working for Wilson Ryder. I told him you were looking for a job, but he didn't say anything."

"You don't have to do me any favors, Ricky," I said. "I don't need Clarance's charity or yours."

"You need somethin'," Ricky declared.

He wanted me to take up the bait and fight or make a joke out of it or anything. But I just stuck out my lower lip and shrugged. I didn't have the energy for that kind of talk right then. I focused my attention on Narciss. She was writing down notes on slips of yellow paper, which she attached to different pieces. She also made entries in a small spiral pad she had.

"Hey, Charles?" Ricky said.

"Hey what?"

"Could I use your phone?"

"Local or long distance?"

"I wanna call Bethany. She said that —"

"Okay," I said, cutting him off. "Make your call."

Ricky gave me a sullen look and then went into the kitchen to use the ancient Princess phone in there. I heard him say Bethany's name and then I returned my attention to Narciss.

She seemed extremely competent. Now and then she'd take some reference book or another from her shoulder satchel to prove or disprove some point she was making to herself. She would write more notes and then move on to the next object. In the meanwhile Ricky was laughing and chattering on the phone in the other room.

I was having a fine time in the chilly window seat, watching the earth-toned woman judge my lineage. The moon shone on her, glaring over my shoulder.

"Are you hungry?" I asked Narciss after it was completely dark outside.

"I'd like something after I'm done here," she said.

"We could go over to Dinelli's in Southampton," I offered and immediately I was sorry. I didn't have a single paper dollar to my name. I probably didn't have enough in change to cover a dinner at Dinelli's, and my only credit card had been canceled more than a year before.

"That would be nice," Narciss Gully said.

She turned back to her work, and I jumped up to go to the kitchen.

"Be right back," I promised.

Ricky was cradling the phone with both hands against his face. His voice was low, and I knew that he must have been getting somewhere with Bethany Baptiste. Bethany was a heavyset young woman who liked food, dancing, and men.

She could never get enough of any one of them, and we all loved her for it.

She'd been married once but that didn't take. Bethany married Lawrence Crelde, but she was in love with Clarance, who was already married. Whenever Clarance called, Bethany came running, and one day when she got back, Lawrence was gone. Bethany wasn't upset about losing her husband, but she was devastated when Clarance refused to leave his own wife for her.

Ever since then Bethany was alone. She'd go out with this man or that for a few days or weeks, but something always got in the way. Right now it looked like Ricky was going to be her date. At any other time I would have sat back and waited for him to finish with his line, but right then I had my own troubles.

"Ricky," I said.

He waved at me to go away.

"Ricky," I said a little louder.

Again he waved.

"Get off the phone, man. I have to talk to you."

"It's Charles Blakey," he said into the mouthpiece. And then after listening to something, he said to me, "Bethany says hey."

"Tell her that you have to talk to me for a minute."

"Let me call you back in five?" he said. Whatever she said must have been promising because Ricky smiled and whispered something so soft that I couldn't make it out.

"What you want, Charles? Damn. Here I am tryin' to promote somethin' an' you all up in my face."

"I got to have forty bucks, man. Got to have it."

"Charles . . ."

"No, Ricky. No games. No fuckin' around. I don't have a single dollar bill, but Narciss wants to eat."

"Who cares what that skinny bitch want?"

"Sh!" I was worried that she might hear us even though we were whispering. "I care."

All of a sudden Ricky was sly. He let his eyes almost close and then he nodded. "I see," he said.

"I'll pay you back the minute this stuff is sold. Fifty dollars for forty."

Ricky reached into his pocket and pulled out a roll of twenty-dollar bills. He must have had six hundred dollars in his hand. He smiled and peeled off two bills. He handed them over and then grinned again.

"You got what you want now, brother?" he asked me.

"Thanks," I said.

"Well then, can I get back on the phone and get what I need?"

Ricky was crooning to Bethany before I had left the room.

I found Narciss holding up a lopsided pink glass vase.

She was scrutinizing every aspect of the vessel like a budget shopper studying a possible buy from an overcrowded reject table.

I sat there with knots in my stomach. It made me sick to have to ask Ricky for charity. And watching Narciss sift through my family's history now somehow made me sad. The cold from the window worked its way into my gut. I wondered if I was getting sick.

"Oh my," Narciss said.

"What?"

Instead of answering she came to me with a wooden box held delicately in both her hands. She sat down next to me, placing the old scarred box between us. Other than its obvious age, it was unremarkable. About a foot long and six inches in depth and width, it was plain and held together by smith-made iron hinges. There were three letters roughly carved on the lower right side of the lid — JLD.

"Look." She lifted the lid.

Inside there were three hand-carved masks, rust to dark brown, ivory I was sure. Each one was about five inches from crown to chin and three inches from one cheekbone to the other. They were simple images with sloping foreheads and slitted eyes. One was smiling, one possibly feral, and one looked like he was whistling through an O-shaped mouth. They were laid out on an old crumpled newspaper. Two of the faces had been broken in places but were seamed back together with some kind of adhesive. There was a blue splotch on the delicate chin of the leftmost image. They were beautiful and commanding, fitting perfectly in the wood box that, I supposed, was built to hold them.

"It's the history of your history," Narciss whispered.

The words came to me as truth. I believed I was looking at the cargo, carried on some European ship, of an African who had sold himself into indentured servitude. Maybe they were his gods, carved by some uncle.

"Touch them," Narciss said like an impatient lover showing a virgin the ropes.

Instead I closed the box and took a deep breath. When I put down the lid, the music stopped. Not real music but something that played in my mind. Something high-pitched but soft and repeating like a squeaky woodwind playing its rendition of cascading water.

My intestines grew colder and a spasm wanted to run down my spine but did not. I clutched Narciss's forearm for support and took another deep breath.

"Tell me about the rest of this stuff," I said.

She had to disengage from my grip to look at her spiral

pad. She said a lot of stuff about quality and pedigree, condition of resins and uniqueness in the market. She talked about the market a lot, but I didn't understand most of it. It was just good to hear her talking. So self-assured and serious. Every beat was a word and every word meant something. Maybe I didn't understand, but I hoped to, I wanted to.

"So?" she asked. "What do you think?"

"About what?"

"Is there something wrong, Mr. Blakey?"

Just then Ricky broke out into loud laughter. I looked toward the kitchen and then back to Narciss.

"Why do you ask that?"

"I don't know," she said with a frown. "You seem distracted. When I came you were sitting in that window in the dark, and you seemed like you . . . you were in a daze. But I think I understand."

"Well if you do I hope you let me in on it."

She smiled at my helplessness and said, "I'm sure that all of this digging into your family history has made you very upset. Bringing it all out. Thinking about selling it off. It must feel like selling your soul, or even worse, selling your ancestors' souls."

Again what she said cut right into me. I was beginning to fear her words.

"It's just stuff," I said. "Something that's been in the basement. I didn't even know I had most of it. I would have thrown it away if it wasn't for Ricky."

"It might be better that way," she said. "At least if you threw away the spirit of your heritage, you wouldn't make it into merchandise."

"Are you trying to talk me out of this?" I asked the slender brown woman.

"I'm sorry, Mr. Blakey. You know, I come to the antique business through school. I got my B.A. at Penn with a double major in anthropology and archaeology. Then I went to RISD for a graduate degree in textiles. Everything I know about antiques comes from the inside out. It's more than a business with me; it's a way to see our history. And I thought maybe you had the same feelings when you got so low."

"Hey, hey, hey," I said again in that low voice. "I'm sorry. This is all new to me. But you know I've got to sell this stuff. Even if it's something important and I don't know it. Maybe we could find some people like you to appreciate what they got. How much do you think it's worth?"

"That depends," she said. "If the paintings have artistic value, which I doubt, they could go pretty high. But I think I can authenticate the dates they were done and the artist, Blythe Blakey-Richards, and so I'm sure there are some museums and universities that would have at least an anthropological interest. The furniture is Arts and Crafts and earlier. The clothes have museum possibilities, and there are also some collectors. The toys and tools might be the most valuable items. I would try to sell them to dealers. The whole lot, with the exception of the masks, might bring in anywhere from forty to a hundred thousand. Probably closer to forty."

"Damn." That was Ricky. He was standing in the doorway to the kitchen. "Four gees just for knowing who should shake hands. That's what I need to do for a livin'."

He rubbed his hands together and grinned. "You'all can tell me the damage later. Right now I got to go see somebody. Have a nice dinner."

Ricky shook my hand, maybe for the first time ever, and he kissed Narciss on the cheek. Then he danced out the front door, full of the expectations of Bethany's charms.

When he was gone I asked, "So how do we do this?"

"I'll come over with a camera and photograph everything. You'll get a copy of each image. I'll give you a receipt for the items and have them moved to a room above my shop in Bridgehampton. Then I begin to invite buyers. As I sell off items, I pass on the proceeds to you — minus expenses and twenty percent."

"Twenty? I thought you got ten."

"Richard wants me to retain his fee also. I said I would, but if you have a problem with that —"

"No, no, no. That's okay. So how soon before I see some money?"

"Well, let me see. I'm going on a buying trip starting tomorrow that will last for ten days. One day for the photographing and delivery. Then I have to e-mail, call, or write to the right clients. The museums may take months to get back to me —"

"Months?"

"— but many of the dealers are around here and so I'll probably start getting something in a month to six weeks."

I wondered how soon the bank would move in to try to foreclose on the bad debt. I was already more than a month late in my payments. I needed at least twelve hundred dollars to get the debtors off my back. For a moment I wondered if I could get an advance from Narciss. It was worth a try, but I couldn't get the words out. I didn't want her to see me begging.

"It's a little late for dinner," I said. "I'm tired from all of this work. Can we make it the day you come for photographs?"

The momentary shadow of sadness across her face made me glad that I hadn't asked for the advance.

"Oh sure," she said. "I understand. This kind of work is exhausting not only physically but also in your heart." She reached out and curled her long finger around my forearm. It was meant to be supportive and it was successful.

"Mr. Blakey?"

"Uh-huh."

"Keep the masks with you for a while. For at least a year."

"Don't you want to study them? To figure out how old they are and where they're from?"

"It's more important that you keep something that has your roots in it. You should sleep next to them and feel their presence. No amount of study will take the place of your family's heart."

She leaned forward. I could feel the breath from her nostrils on my arm. The way she looked at me held a question, a request. I knew it was her desire for me to keep the masks, but that wish called up another whole feeling in me.

She moved back and whispered, "You're a sweet man."

I wanted to kiss her but she moved too quickly, putting on her jacket and hefting her shoulder bag. When I approached she stuck out a hand at me. All I could do was shake and say goodbye.

nine

The next few days went by quickly. I spent them scrubbing and cleaning the basement. I also straightened up the house as well as I could. The walls and floors of the basement needed paint, but all I had was forty dollars, so elbow grease was the only oil-based liquid I used.

My uncle Brent used to say that I was lazy and worthless. He said it whenever my mother was out.

"I'm surprised that a boy like you don't starve 'cause he too lazy to lift the fork to his lips," he said often. And then he'd laugh in a wheezing manner and I'd wish that he'd fall down the steps and die.

I hated everything about Brent. The fact that he talked in a southern Negro dialect made me hate his kind of blackness. I didn't want to be associated with *street*. You had to prove yourself to me if you didn't speak like an educated person, a white person. When Ricky came back from Brooklyn, I didn't like him because I heard the whispering, muttering southern talk of Brent in his words. Even then, in that room, fourteen years after Brent had died, I was still angry at him.

"You stupid fuck," I said to a memory. "Dumb shit motherfucker. I'll kill you."

Sometimes I'd spend the whole day walking around the house cursing Brent and all the mean things he said. At odd moments his name would come to my lips with some new curse to level at him. It was like he was still alive and I was in my late teens, forced to care for him after burying my own mother.

He was bedridden by that time. A nurse came in from social services and Medicare, but I was still expected to feed him and give him some of his drugs. I was never late or forgetful because my mother made me promise before she died that I would take care of him.

But that didn't mean I had to talk. I walked into that room with his tray, sullen and closemouthed. He tried to be friendly, but I couldn't bring myself to speak. I blamed Brent for everything that ever befell me. My father's death, my mother's, the feeling I had that I couldn't tie my shoes right — all of that I blamed Brent for. Even when he looked pitiful and small, I hated him. The skin on his face was brittle and creased. He resembled the center mask in the set — a crack down the forehead to the lips.

At night in those last days, I would dream about Brent. In the dream I cried over his suffering. But the next morning, when I brought in his soft-boiled egg, my heart hardened again.

I spent three days cursing Brent and cleaning up years of squalor. At night I'd buy a cheap pint of Greenly's Gin and drink it, but only after 10:00 — only after I'd read and eaten and done everything that I had to do. I wanted to cut down on the booze because of Clarance and Narciss. Clarance because he thought he was mad at me but really what he was mad at was me from tipsy to drunk. I get mean with alcohol.

When I'm high I think I'm being funny, but I knew that Clarance hated being called Clara. I knew it.

And Narciss thought I was sweet. She thought I was something sensitive and discriminating. Maybe if I stayed sober for a while, I'd become a better person; maybe I could make something out of myself.

Anniston Bennet came on Friday at 4:00 exactly. He wore yellow short sleeves over a blue T-shirt, and brown trousers. His tennis shoes were the same blue as his shirt. He had no tie and the yellow shirt was open at the throat, showing a hairy pale neck over the top of the T-shirt collar. His head was oval and his chin came to a tip like the masks that I kept in their box on the windowsill next to my bed. His blue eyes were a perpetual shock, but there was no wonder or magic in the rest of his face.

"Mr. Blakey," he said, extending a hand over the threshold. His small hand held a surprisingly strong grip.

"Mr. Bennet. Come in."

"You're house cleaning?" Bennet asked as we went through the living room that was crowded with the refuse of my ancestors.

"Cleaned out the cellar." I led my guest into the nook off the kitchen. There was a round maple table there with three chairs. The window looked out into a stone yard, fenced in by vine-covered trellises. The ground was tiled with broad slabs of mossy granite plates. Sunlight dappled in through the slat roof.

I thought such a beautiful sight would jack up any price that the white man was willing to pay. But he barely noticed the view.

"Do you want some cola or lemonade?" I had shopped for this meeting. I also had crackers, French bread, and Parma ham if he was hungry.

"No, thank you," he said without gratitude. "Can we see the cellar now?"

I led him out the back door and to the entrance in the ground. I threw the trapdoor open and stepped aside, indicating that he should go first. I'd left the light on so he would have no trouble descending the stairs. But he hesitated, even took a step backward. Then, with a visible force of will, he steeled himself and walked down the sixteen stairs.

I followed.

He glanced furtively from one corner to the other, then up to the ceiling and back to the stairs. He squinted but the light wasn't bright. He clapped his hands together, took a deep breath.

I said, "Cellar's got running water, but there's no toilet down there, Mr. —"

"First let me tell you," he interrupted, "that I have particular requests. I want to rent this cellar for sixty-five days, starting on July one. I will remain here for the whole time, and I expect no one to enter except for you. You will prepare and bring food and you will dispose of any materials that need disposing of. Everything else I need will be delivered two weeks before I am due to arrive. With that will come instructions for any construction necessary."

"So you want me to be your cook and butler?"

"Not exactly, but that's close enough to the truth."

"I'm sorry, Mr. Bennet, but —"

"I will pay all expenses, plus seven hundred and fifty dollars a day."

The math stopped me in my tracks. Zero times, five times, seven times. "Forty-eight thousand seven hundred fifty dollars," I said.

Anniston Bennet smiled. Math done right seemed to please him.

He was uncomfortable in the basement, however.

"Let's go back up," he said, leading the way up the stairs.

I didn't understand how he could be so anxious to rent that room if he couldn't bear five minutes there.

Back in the breakfast room, he regained his composure.

"I will give you eight thousand five hundred right now as a deposit and then on June fifteen you will receive what paraphernalia I will need for my recluse. You will follow any instructions I have given, and then I will arrive at midnight of June thirty. At that time, after I have inspected the work, I will give you twenty thousand dollars, plus another five for expenses. Sixty-five days later I will give you the balance. All moneys will be in cash."

Tiny shafts of sunlight shone on Bennet's head and his small hands, which were folded on the table in front of him. He was unchanged by the light. I realized that the insecurity and friendliness he'd shown on our first meeting were an act.

"Man so cold," my uncle Brent would say of evil white men, "that he could take a bath in ice water and still take his whiskey on the rocks."

"Well?" Bennet asked.

"What if . . . " I stalled. "What if I just take your money and then say I didn't?"

The smile this time was a memory of some previous event. "In my experience, Mr. Blakey, people rarely renege on their promises. It's always easier to keep your word than to enter into lies or intrigue."

Looking back on it I should have been scared by his words, but instead I was confused. I wondered what point of view could see honesty as the stronger virtue in a world I knew was full of cheating and lies. Didn't they lie in commercials on TV and ads in newspapers? Didn't politicians lie about what they've done and what they're about to do? Clarance lied all the time to his wife, and he had more girlfriends than I did.

But then I thought about Narciss and how the truth had been so easy with her.

"You say you're going to lie to the government, not tell them about the money," I said.

"The government isn't real," he replied. He might have been talking about Santa Claus or God. "I don't owe anything to anyone who in themselves are lies and liars."

Talking to the white man made me very nervous. There were all these thoughts in my head. Thoughts about love and lies and money. Especially money. Money and the mortgage and food and work. I had been calling around about jobs for days, but no one wanted to hire me except for a McDonald's out on the highway and the plastics factory in Riverhead. But those jobs were part-time and minimum wage. No way I could pay my bills with that.

"Why did you come to me, Mr. Bennet? Of all the places out here, how did you choose my house?"

"I had an associate of mine question Teddy Odett. My friend was looking for a place that I could go. He knew my requirements and asked Odett and also Minder at the bank in town what my best options were. As you know, you can't find a job around here and your mortgage is in arrears. My offer settles your problems and gives me what I need." Bennet's words and his bright blue eyes were pure and innocent. But what he was telling me was that a stranger could walk into my life and find out more about me than my closest family and friends ever knew.

"How do you make your money, Mr. Bennet?"

"I'm an agent for a consortium of investment and oil companies. I do research and reclamation work all through the world."

"Reclaiming what?"

"Wealth." He said the word and it tickled him.

"No drugs or anything?"

He shook his head. His hands hadn't moved and the sunlight now shone on his forearms.

"You got the money on you?"

"In a brown paper bag in my trunk," he said.

"So you hand over the money and I just wait for your furniture and stuff?"

He nodded.

"You really found out about my mortgage and house and everything?"

"I'm a man who gets what he wants, Mr. Blakey. I want your cellar and I'm willing to give you what you need."

I couldn't see anything wrong with a man wanting to be a monk. I certainly didn't have any problems with fifty thousand dollars. But there was something, some formality, an expectation from Bennet that made me feel this *recluse*, as he called it, was more than just a vacation or retreat. I wanted to find the right question to ask, to pull out the truth that he professed to believe in.

But I felt that it couldn't go on much longer. If I said no that day, then my chances would be over. The bank wouldn't give a petty embezzler a break on the mortgage. I couldn't work.

"What do you plan to be doing down there in my basement?" I asked.

"Reading, thinking. If I get the opportunity maybe I'll do some writing."

"Nothing else?"

"Eat and sleep." Bennet's face was reposed and patient. He even gave me a wan smile.

"What do you mean, *if you get the opportunity?*"

"Many things depend on circumstance, Mr. Blakey. Opportunities stem from these circumstances."

I was beaten by this last interchange. Anniston Bennet wanted to live the hermit's life in a two-hundred-year-old cellar. I needed the money. I tried to think about what my mother would advise, but all I could come up with was a sad face and a deep sigh, a beseeching look that said I hoped I did right. Uncle Brent would have damned me for either choice.

I wanted to say no, but instead I said, "Okay, Mr. Bennet. Bring me your paper bag and we have a deal."

The white man handed me the bag and shook my hand in the street in front of my house. Irene Littleneck watched and smoked over our exchange.

"See you on July one," Bennet said softly.

"You bet."

Again he got into his turquoise Volkswagen, made a U-turn, and drove off. Irene met my eye from her porch across the street. She probably wanted an explanation. I had known her since I was a child — getting into mischief and having my ears twisted by her and her sister, Chastity.

"How is Chastity, Miss Littleneck?" I hailed.

"Restin'," the aged woman replied.

"Give her my best," I said.

"Thank you," Irene said, and she turned off the heavy stare of accusation. A kind word about her family always softened her punishing ways.

ten

I answered the phone after it had been ringing for a very long time.

"Helah," I said.

"Charles? Charles, are you awake?"

It was Monday morning and I was sprawled out on the floor in front of the couch in the living room. My pillow was a paper bag that held almost eight thousand dollars on top of a brand-new boom box that I'd picked up in East Hampton. Next to me was a half-empty bottle of Courvoisier. A cognac high is the smoothest thing in the world. Even the hangover is like being squeezed by a velvet vise.

"Ricky? Ricky, what time is it?"

"It's afternoon, Charles. Afternoon." As wild as Ricky thought he was, he was still a blue-collar man. The thought of sleeping during daylight hours was sinful to him.

"What you want, Ricky?"

"My mom got back home from her sister's last night."

"Yeah? Tell her hello for me," I said. Ricky's mother had always been kind to me.

"Yeah, okay. But listen. Bethany wanna come over tonight,

you hear what I'm sayin'? She got a roommate and I got my mom."

"Doesn't she have a room?" When I sat up, a spasm went through my intestines. For a moment I thought I was going to vomit right there on my money.

"Yeah, man, but the kinda lovin' she spoons out is too loud for a small apartment." I could hear the greed in Ricky's voice. "Let us stay with you tonight? You know —the same deal you used to make with Clarance."

I saw a hawk through the window. She was stiff-winged and wheeling round.

A huntress, I thought, *honing in on her prey*.

The thought chilled me, and I forgot for a moment or two about Ricky on the other end of the line.

"You could keep the fifty you owe me," he said.

"I got your fifty right here in my wallet, man."

"Where you get that?"

I rose to my feet, holding the bag of money in my right hand.

"Yeah, you two could stay," I said. "I'll even make you dinner."

I spent the day taking care of business. I went to the bank in Southampton and gave them four payments on the mortgage, in cash. I paid ahead on the rest of my utilities too. I bought groceries that would last a month or more. That included six quarts of cheap bourbon — I didn't want to waste any more money on cognac. I also bought paint, paintbrushes, tools, and every kind of cleaning liquid, brush, and rag. I bought three pairs of jeans, a pair of Timberjack work boots, four checkered flannel shirts, and a new toothbrush. I renewed my subscription to the *New York Times*, partially because I thought Bennet would want to read it, and bought four CDs of Thelonious Sphere Monk, whose music was the only thing in the world that Brent and I both loved.

I went to the used bookstore in the Harbor and bought fifteen sci-fi hardbacks. Mostly Philip K. Dick and Brian Aldiss. I was digging in for the long haul. This was mainly due to the fear that I'd waste all the money Bennet gave me before I had taken care of business.

Brent used to say that money went through my fingers like water down the drain. He wasn't wrong. The first thing I did when Bennet left was to go out and buy a pure gold ring that I had seen in an antique store in East Hampton. It was a slender thing with a pale green stone for a setting. It was from India, Mrs. Canelli said. It was a woman's ring and too small for me, but I wanted it anyway. And once I had the money, I couldn't help myself.

My mother gave me my allowance every Saturday morning, and I'd spend the rest of the day shopping for candy and gifts for her.

"Don't spend everything, baby," she'd tell me. But her eyes were alight whenever I'd bring out a bottle of perfume or some glass trinket.

By the time Ricky and Bethany arrived, I was making dinner. Hot and sweet Italian sausages fried with whole cloves of garlic and then simmered in red wine and tomato sauce. The water for the vermicelli had just come to a boil when Ricky and Bethany came in. She was a few inches taller and almost twice the size of Ricky, but Bethany wasn't fat. She had a big chest and powerful legs, but the stomach was flat. Her face was wide and the color of dark amber. She had big teeth, an embarrassing laugh, and eyes that glittered when they saw you.

"Hey, Charles," she called. They had let themselves in the front door. "That smells delicious. You got some for us?"

"I didn't know if you guys had time to eat. From what Ricky said I thought you were real tired and had to go to bed."

"Uh-uh," she denied. "We came to see you and eat some sausages too."

She put her arms around me and gave me a kiss that made me hug her back.

"Let's eat!" Ricky declared. And for a while I had some company and no thoughts in my head.

Bethany loved eating and sex, as I have said before, but she also loved to talk about herself. We heard all about her plans of moving down to Atlanta and starting a braid-and-nail parlor. She loved children and had gone to some wild parties at crazy artists' homes in Southampton. One well-known painter had asked her to model three times, but every time he was so moved by her ample beauty that he had to make love to her instead.

I could see that most of her stories were designed to excite her male audience. It worked. Ricky was almost swooning over her words. He had run into her at a shopping mall near Riverhead a week or so earlier, and she gave him hopes. Now he was only a sausage away.

"Hey, Bethy," he said.

"Yeah?"

"I wanna show you somethin' upstairs."

"What?" she asked.

"Somethin'."

"You comin', Charles?" Bethany pursed her lips and lowered her eyelids. If we were out in nature, I would have killed Ricky right then.

"In a few minutes," I said.

Ricky sighed in relief.

"Okay," she said, smiling. "But you come on up now."

"I'll be there."

"Come on," Ricky said, grabbing her by the arm.

"Ow! Don't be so rough, Ricky. I'm comin'."

I washed the dishes and looked out the window. I was thinking about Anniston Bennet and the bag of money that I had hidden in the foldout sofa bed in my father's old library. A bagful of money was not a normal thing —that's what I was thinking. No matter how much the little white man had acted like it was a simple business transaction, it was obvious that he wanted to hide what he was doing. It made me nervous, but I couldn't see any way out of it. Twenty-five hundred dollars of the money was already gone.

But how bad could it be? He couldn't hurt anybody in my basement. He was just little so I knew he couldn't hurt me. Unless he had a gun. But I could lock the doors while he was down there. Of course a man with a gun could get through a door, or a window.

But why would he need to pay me money? Why not just shoot me in the breakfast nook?

"*Ohhhh.*"

I couldn't believe that Bennet had any designs on my welfare. I decided to get drunk and stop worrying about things I couldn't change.

"*Ohhhhh.*" It was only a whisper. But, I thought, it had to be a roar to make it all the way down into the kitchen from my parents' room on the third floor. That was the deal I usually made with Clarance. He could come to my house with one of his girlfriends. They'd stay on the third floor and I'd sleep downstairs in my father's den. But it was the first time that Ricky had asked for the deal.

I never imagined that Bethany, who spoke in a small high voice, could get the volume to disturb me downstairs.

That's when I remembered being a child. Now and then my parents wanted to be alone, *to talk*, they said. They'd go into their room and tell me to go play. But all I wanted was to play with them and talk to them. After they sent me away from the door a few times, I'd wander down to the pantry with my toy soldiers and guns. I was happy then because there was a vent that let me hear my parents' soft murmuring voices while I played soldier.

"That's it, baby," Bethany said. She might have been talking to me, her voice was so clear. "Right there. Right there. Right there."

Ricky was saying something, and she replied with a whole drawerful of yeses.

I hadn't masturbated in three days because of the alcohol. By the time I got around to that, I was too dizzy to do anything. Bethany was telling Ricky where to move and when he got it right she let go with a strained roar.

That was my first orgasm too.

I could hear the furniture rocking and Bethany's squeals. She knew what she wanted and was very specific in her requests. To hear a woman ask for pleasure like that had me on my knees among the boxes of cereal and plastic containers of grape juice. After my third orgasm I had to leave the pantry for the living room. There I began to drink. It was necessary to slow down my beating heart.

From the sofa I could hear the occasional moan or gasping sob, but the whiskey dulled my urges and I fell half into a doze.

"Charles?" she said. "You awake?"

I was asleep on the couch in the living room. At least I think I was asleep. It seemed to me that I had been looking at Bethany in her tight satin slip for quite some time.

"Are you awake?"

"Uh-huh."

"Ricky's asleep," she said as if it was an important piece of information.

She sat down next to me and I got up, almost without thinking, and moved to the chair. That made Bethany smile.

"You scared of me, Charles Blakey?" she asked.

"You know a lot of those rich people come in here from New York, don't you, Bethy?" I asked.

She was confused by my changing her subject but still answered, "Some."

"They do some crazy things, right?"

"I guess," she said. "I mean, they think they're all crazy and wild. And they don't have to get up and go to work in the morning. Really all the difference I can see is that they think that they're smarter and better than people don't make as much money as they do. And they want a lot more. You know, like that artist I used to go with. He wanted to be the best at everything. And he was so rich that everybody told him that he was the best. When he started playing trumpet, his friends said that he sounded like Miles Davis. It wasn't like us. You know somebody set you straight in a minute around here."

Bethany smiled and I wanted to kiss her, not because she was beautiful, even though she was, but because she wasn't impressed by the lies rich people wore like clothes. She knew where her feet were planted. Right then I think she wanted to be standing a little closer to me.

She stood up and walked over to my chair. I stood to meet her.

71

She was about to lay her hand on my chest, but I took hold of her wrist and gently pushed her away.

"I want to see you, Bethy," I said. "But not downstairs from Ricky after you made him all happy like that."

"We could take a shower," she suggested.

"It's not that. You know Ricky can get low and dirty, but he's the only friend I got right now. Believe me, this is not easy. But can I make you some tea?"

Bethany frowned for a few seconds, and then she shrugged and smiled. There was a sweater on the floor. She must have let it fall from her shoulders when she saw me slouching on the couch. Now she picked it up and covered all that youthful beauty.

Over Irish Breakfast (it was 4:30) we discussed the rich white people she'd known. Bethany liked the fine dinners and fancy houses, but rich people — even the black ones, she said — couldn't satisfy her like people from our neighborhood.

"It's just like my people know me better," she said. "Like Ricky. You know for a while tonight I thought he might have a heart attack, he was so excited. And before he fell off asleep he was talking about Johnetta Johnston and Kirby. You know? Everyday stuff. Rich men always want to be teaching something, asking, *Did you know?* when they know you don't know and don't care neither."

Ricky came down when the sun was just coming up. At first he looked suspicious, but when Bethany showed him her big teeth and said, "Mornin', baby. Charles made me some tea," he calmed down and kissed her face and neck.

After that they went back upstairs. I was so tired that I didn't even listen. I went to sleep with my bag of money in my dead father's foldout sofa and dreamed about Anniston

Bennet. He was humongous and wedged tight in my cellar, sticking his head out of the trapdoor and begging to be let free.

eleven

I spent the next week working on the basement and reading the books I had bought. Late every afternoon Ricky would call to crow about his further conquests with Bethany. One night they did it on the beach. The next night in an almost-empty movie house. Late late every night Bethany would call me. She just wanted to talk, she'd say. Every conversation would end with her worrying that Ricky was too much in love with her. She liked him and he was sweet, but he wasn't the kind of man who could ring that bell. Twice she wondered if she could come over in those wee hours, but every time I was strong.

"I'd like to see you," I said. "I really would, but Ricky likes you and I can't see it to break his heart."

"What if we broke up?" she asked me one night. "Could I come over then?"

"I don't know."

"'Cause you know it seem like that if you didn't wanna hurt Ricky you'd let me come over and just not tell 'im. That way nobody gets hurt."

I told her that I would think about what she said.

I didn't care about Bethany and Ricky right then. The next morning Narciss Gully was due to come over to take the photographs. I had spent the day cleaning again. Actually I just moved whatever mess had collected into the pantry. I didn't drink for twenty-four hours previous to her arrival, and I took a long bath and shaved.

When the doorbell rang I wasn't expecting the twenty-something copper-toned Dominican Adonis of assistants.

"Hola," he said to me. "I am Geraldo. Miss Gully sent me to set up for the shoot."

I'm tall but Geraldo had me beat. He was six four at least, wearing only cutoff jean shorts and a white T-shirt. His muscles were well defined but not grotesque, except for calves that bulged. His hair came in big golden-brown locks. His face was beautiful.

"Huh?" I said.

"Preparation," he said slowly, taking time over the syllables. He indicated a pile of paraphernalia behind him. Lighting, screens, rugs, and big camera boxes. "See?"

"Oh. Uh-huh. Yeah. Why don't you come in here in the living room?"

Geraldo lifted the great pile of materials into a rippling embrace and carried it in. I showed him where to set up, and he spent a long time with a light meter looking at windows in order to find the exact right position for his rugs and screens. He examined my heirlooms, holding them up to the light and using his meter.

"Are you taking the pictures?" I asked after a lot of watching.

The boyish smile and manly shaking of his head must have broken many hearts before. "No," he said. "Miss Gully takes the pictures. I just set it up."

"You work for her?"

"We are friends. She loves my work, my painting, and so she gives me jobs when she can. I live at the house of Harry Lake in East Hampton. He is my master in oils. A great master. He sent for me from New York after seeing my show at the Rhinoceros Gallery on Avenue A. Do you know it?"

"Know what?"

"The Rhinoceros Gallery. It is a very important place. Harry found me there, and he lets me use his garage as a studio and to sleep."

"So how do you know Narciss?" I asked.

"I was walking down the street," he said, tossing his locks for effect. "Just walking and I see the most beautiful quilts hanging in her window. The designs are like the ones that I paint and I had to see them, touch them..."

There was a passion building up in Geraldo, and I couldn't help but wonder what all he was touching up in Narciss Gully's store.

"I know," I said for no reason, "she sells quilts."

"Sells?" he sneered. "It's not a hot-dog stand. This is art. She collects, she shares, she teaches. Sometimes someone might pay for learning something, to live with beauty. But she does not just sell quilts."

I've never really gotten the knack of talking to artists. You can't talk to them about how much it pays or about what you think you like. If I think a painting is ugly, somebody just tells me that I don't understand. If I think a painting is good, they tell me the same thing. It's like artists see a different place, a higher place, whereas I'm on the level of some stray dog who only knows how to hunt for pussy and food in a world that's black and white.

Geraldo sneered at me again and turned to his work.

I considered kicking him out of my house but then thought better of it. I didn't want trouble with Narciss Gully. Just the opposite — I had begun to have deep feelings for the antique dealer. Every night after talking to Bethany, I would have lascivious dreams about Narciss. In those dreams we always started at the dinner table, either in a restaurant or at someone's house, maybe a barbecue or a picnic. No matter where we ended up, we always started out eating. I'd bring the wine and she was barely dressed. She was shy about her small breasts and slender thighs, but I would console her by stroking her body and rubbing my face against her magnificent skin. In these dreams my excitement grew and grew, but always before we could embrace, something happened to interrupt. The waiter would arrive with the check, a downpour fell on our picnic, someone would come to the door — her mother or Clarance wanting to apologize. No matter who it was I'd get so angry that I'd wake up with a powerful erection. Awake, I couldn't recapture the ardor of my dreams. And without passion there was no desire for the consummation of my lust.

"Mr. Blakey?" She had come in behind me while I watched her assistant and thought of her.

"Oh," I said. "Hi, Narciss."

"Hello, Geraldo," she said, having satisfied her social obligation with me. "Have you been here long?"

"Not long," the godling reported to his muse. He was holding up a terrible painting done by my aunt Blythe. "Is this really worth the film?"

"We'll do the paintings first," she said. "And after that the clothes and then the hard objects."

The crestfallen look on Geraldo's face was worth a whole week of hard labor.

"Excuse us, Mr. Blakey, but we're going to be working in here for a while."

"If you call me Charles, I'll let you alone."

She smiled without answering and I left, grinning broadly at the sour-faced Geraldo.

The next few hours were tough for me. I was reading a book but wanting a drink. The book was about a prince who had been stripped of his memory and exiled from a magical kingdom to mundane Earth. There were agents trying to kill him, but in his confused state he couldn't understand why. I liked the story because I often felt like that, like I was being persecuted but didn't know why. Why was I alive and seeing and thinking and dreaming if everything was just stoplights and televisions, tests and failures, red wine and death?

But I didn't want a drink to escape, not then anyway. I needed a drink because I wanted to ask Narciss for that rain check for the dinner we'd missed.

The first obstacle would be asking the question in the presence of the adoring Geraldo's imposing physique. But I got over that. I could see that Narciss wasn't all that interested in the Dominican artist. When he strutted and preened, she hardly noticed. He was actually just an assistant.

But even when I saw that he was no competitor, I still held back.

After being nearly crushed to death and then incarcerated in a mental hospital, the prince escaped and was running. I decided to go in and check on my guests.

"How's it going?" I asked, entering the room.

Geraldo sneered but Narciss took off her glasses and smiled.

"We're halfway through it," she said. "It's taking longer than usual because I'm taking a separate slide shot. Some of these pieces are so wonderful that I'll have to send them for projection."

"Oh," I said. "Good. Good. Would you like to get d-dinner after this?"

Just that one small stammer made me want to bite off my tongue. One double skip on the letter *d* and I'd told Narciss all about my fears and weaknesses. Geraldo was standing behind me, but I'm sure he was grinning at my failed manhood. The smile on Narciss's lips I took to be pity and pleasure at the discomfort of a child.

"I'm sorry, Charles, but I have plans," she said.

"Uh-huh." I nodded, putting an upbeat tone to the grunt and realizing too late that that made me sound even more pitiable.

"But maybe we can have coffee or something after we're finished here. There are a couple of things that we need to discuss."

"No problem. Just as long as we're through before seven 'cause you know I got to get out and eat something." Every word out of my mouth seemed calculated to make me look more like a fool.

I went back into the kitchen feeling as if I were descending into a pit. Every step brought me lower. And all it was was just that double *d*. A stuttering skip and my fingers were tingling, the light in the room refused to illuminate. I didn't feel hungry; I didn't want a drink. My months of unemployment, my loneliness, my drunken poverty all came to the surface then. I would have liked to cry but I couldn't. The prince in my novel was reduced to a mass of unreadable words.

The minutes went by and I kept sinking. At some point Narciss came in. She had sent Geraldo away, but I didn't care. She wanted coffee and I made it, but the brew was unbearably weak and she took no more than a sip.

"Are you okay?" she asked. "I mean, you look kind of sad."

"Fine," I said.

"Is this a good time to talk?"

"Sure."

"It's about those masks." Narciss was excited. She took a large book from her shoulder bag and opened it. Because I didn't move my head, she pulled her chair next to mine and opened to a page marked by a red ribbon. On the page was a carven mask that resembled the three masks on my windowsill.

"Passport masks," she said. "That's what this is and it's also what we found in that box. They were used as identification but also as a way of bringing home along with you when you were away on a long journey. It's hard to say, but the masks you have could represent a family, maybe three brothers or friends who set sail for America as indentured servants. The majority of passport masks are made of wood, so the fact that these are ivory might have special significance."

"Uh-huh," I said because she seemed to be waiting for some kind of response.

"They might have belonged to rich men, maybe even royalty. Your family might descend from a direct bloodline of *kings*." The emphasis she put on *kings* was dramatic and full of feeling.

But if I was a prince, I too had forgotten.

"I'm getting hungry." It was almost impossible for me to get out those few words. "Why don't you write me or call about the stuff, you know, that you're selling."

"But these masks —"

"I have to talk about it later. Later."

I was looking at the book, the picture of a longish face carved from wood. The eyes were gouged out, making a ridge for the nose. The forehead was high and the mouth was just a slit. Narciss's hands closed the book and then pulled it away. I heard her chair sliding backward. As she moved away the air on that side seemed to cool, as if her body heat had been keeping me warm.

I didn't want her to go but I couldn't even look up — much less ask her to stay.

"The boy so retarded he sit on the toilet waitin' for inspiration to wipe his ass." That's what my uncle Brent used to say about me on report-card day four times a year.

That's how I felt.

I heard the front door close.

My descent progressed even though I didn't move a muscle for a very long time.

PART TWO

twelve

I closed the windows and locked the front and back doors at 3:00 in the morning. I snapped the phone connections out of the wall and moved the masks down into my father's library. I slept with the money and the masks for a day and a half. People came to the front door but I didn't answer. Once Ricky came around to the library window and called out my name. After he was gone I connected the phone long enough to call his mother's house and leave a message on his answering machine.

"I'm okay, Ricky," I said. "Just thinking about some stuff, so I need to spend some time alone."

After that I disconnected the phone again and spent almost the next six weeks alone in my house. I only went out for pizzas and whiskey. And as time went by, I had less and less desire to see or speak to anyone.

I got letters, mainly from Bethany. Long yearning letters about wanting to see me and asking what was wrong. Ricky had told her about my phone message, and she said that she was worried about me. Every letter she sent was more intimate and more passionate. They were long letters, ten to twelve pages in a rolling cursive hand. I didn't finish most of them but I got the gist. On week three she broke up with Ricky and wanted to see me. By week five she confessed her love.

"I don't know how it happened, Charlie," she wrote.

> But I love you. I love you more than any other man I have ever
> known. There's something so strong and gentle about you.
> You don't care what people think and you just follow your
> own mind. I don't know what you're doing or thinking right
> now, but I hope when you're ready that you will call me and
> see how deep I feel.

I got a letter from Narciss Gully too.
"Dear Mr. Blakey," she wrote.

> Enclosed you will find a check for six hundred dollars thirty-
> two. This is from the sale of four of your great-aunt's paintings
> to the African American Experience Museum in Charleston,
> South Carolina. They were very excited to obtain these works
> and wish to buy more. First I thought that I would see how
> you felt you were being represented. I tried to get you on the
> phone, but there's never any answer.
>
> I also wanted to apologize about the way I acted at your
> house. I realized afterward that you were saddened over the
> loss of so much of your family's history and that Geraldo and
> I were like invaders in your home. I would like to make it up
> to you by buying you a dinner sometime. I know it seems that
> we're always at cross-purposes when it comes to dinner, but
> I'm sure we can make it work.
>
> Please advise,
> Narciss

I wrote a note in response:

> Dear Ms. Gully,
> You seem to be handling the sales well. Please continue as

you see fit. I've been under the weather lately, but when I revive I will call.

Charles Blakey

Two women wanted to see me. At least they thought they wanted to. In my mind I had convinced myself that it was my unavailability that piqued their interest. If I dared to go out on one date, it would all be over.

I wanted to call both of them. I almost connected the phone two or three times every day. But when the moment came, I lost my nerve.

Bethany even came to the door one night. She rang and knocked and called out my name. But I didn't answer. I just stood at the second-floor window at the top of the stairs and watched until she went away.

Those weeks, I felt, were just a small sample of my whole life up until that time — a waste. I slept and ate and drank according to my own clock. I didn't shave or bathe hardly at all. I read for escape. If I was a brave man I would have probably killed myself.

I was everything that my uncle Brent said that I was, and less. Nothing ever changed and I never got any better or worse.

But then I received Anniston Bennet's boxes, and the world I knew receded like an unfinished novel whose story had become overwrought and tedious.

The truck that came that afternoon was unmarked brown. The burly moving men had a knock that could not be ignored. I came down, expecting the police or maybe the fire department.

Both men wore green work pants and strap undershirts. They were white and at least one of them bore tattoos, but I think that they were both marked up with naked women, knives, and hearts.

"We're supposed to put this delivery in the basement," the blond and balding one said.

"Around the side," I told him.

I was in swimming trunks and tennis shoes. We went around the side and down into the cellar. The men hefted six long flat boxes, one at a time, laying five of them on the floor in the rudimentary pattern of a flower (one flat box in the center and each of the other four parallel to one of the sides). The sixth flat box was laid up against the far wall. These boxes were very heavy. I could tell by the way the men strained when carrying them.

After that they brought in two dozen boxes of various sizes and weights. Finally they delivered a loose-leaf notebook that was vacuum sealed in shiny see-through plastic.

Upon handing me the notebook, the balding blond man said, "Well, that's it."

"Do I sign something?" I asked.

"No signatures, no tips," he replied.

They turned away and climbed out of the cellar. I suppose that they got into their truck and drove back to a garage somewhere in Connecticut near where Anniston Bennet told me he lived. I didn't see them out. Instead I sat on the stairs of the basement and began to read my instructions.

I don't remember what I was doing when the movers came, but I do know I was suffering from a severe hangover. That was gone as soon as I saw the first handwritten page. The notebook contained about thirty of these pages. The paper was unlined but the words followed an equal and rigid pattern from side to side that resembled marching ants — they were so small and even in their progress.

THE CONSTRUCTION OF THE CELL was the headline of the first page. "OPEN BOX #1, THE CENTER FLAT, AND REMOVE THE CARDBOARD," the sentence began. Following the instructions revealed a heavy slatted piece of metal that opened into a nine foot square. The flat steel bands, which were at least a quarter of an inch thick, became a latticework grid. A woman might have gotten her hands through one of the openings, or maybe a small-boned man, but a workman could only get a few fingers through one of those holes. At each angle there was a tie that the book told me would fit the tough-looking little padlocks that I also found in the box.

Box number nine held a heavy rubber mat that fit over the slats. Boxes two through five were the walls of the cage. These were exactly the same in design except that there was, of course, no matting. Also, number five had a small square opening in the front, three feet by three feet. Box number twelve contained the door that was to be fitted into this space. It had conventional bars and was designed to open by lifting it kind of like a portal that some people put on their back doors for pets. The roof of the cell was heavy, but it had been placed in such a way that, with a little oomph, I was able to push it over and on top of the nine-foot-cube cage.

All the walls and top and bottom had loops that fitted together and were designed to be held fast by the little padlocks. Each of the thirty-seven padlocks had a numbered key and a small brass key chain. There was a larger key chain onto which fit all of the smaller keys.

It took a couple of hours to construct the cage, or *cell*, as the instructions called it. The basement was large but that structure dominated the space. The tough metal slats gleamed as if they were brand new. I wondered what kind of animal Bennet would bring with him that was so dangerous it had to be kept in a cage.

There were more instructions but I was tired. I went to the house and ate some frosted cornflakes, and then, on a whim, I went back to the cellar, crawled into the cage, and stretched out. It was an odd sensation. I had never been in jail, but I thought that this was close to the experience of incarceration. The light around me seemed to be teeming, like insects in a swamp, because of the winking between the slats and spaces. The rubber was comfortable enough. There was a certain reassurance to the walls' enclosure. I wondered if this cage was for Anniston's rest. Maybe he was afraid that people would attack him in his sleep. Maybe he just liked the walls.

I wasn't aware of falling into sleep. It was a deep, deep rest. The electric light moving across my face as I shifted around felt like a cloudy afternoon. The silence of my cellar spoke glowingly of eternal rest.

But when I woke up I was disoriented. I had forgotten where I was and the reality of the cell scared me. I jumped to my feet, trying to find a way out. But there was none. At least that's what I thought.

I shouted for help, running from side to side, hitting the walls, but there was no give there. Finally I forced myself to sit down. I was shaking and wondering in spite of the situation how much of the shakes came from whiskey. Then I saw the door. It was down and unlocked, but the fit was snug and I had to push pretty hard to get out.

When I crawled out of the cage, the shakes got even worse. Cold and nauseous, I couldn't rise from my knees. It came to me that I had never known real fear before, that I had lived a whole lifetime in complete safety. But there was no solace in that knowledge. I rolled up into a fetal ball and began to moan. Salty sweat trickled down between my lips. The shuddering music of a mothlike throbbing played along the nerves of my neck.

I don't know how long I stayed like that. It may have been an hour or more. But when the fear subsided, I experienced a release so profound that even breath was an ecstasy of incredible joy.

It was dark outside. The evening was cool and clear. I got into my car and drove out to the beach past Bridgehampton and parked. I walked for hours down along the shore. The ocean played its music and the moon cast shadows through the clouds. My feet were bare and the wet sand was cold, but this was a good thing. I needed sensation in my body to counteract the fear that had not left but simply subsided.

Many miles down from my car, I came to an empty parking lot. It was 2:30 in the morning. There was a phone booth in the lot. Information gave up Bethany's number, and she answered on the fourth ring.

"Hello?"

"Bethany?"

"Hi, Charles," she said, suddenly awake and happy.

I told her about the lot and she knew where it was. She didn't ask how I got there or what I wanted.

"I'll be right there," she said.

I sat on the ground next to the phone and waited.

After nearly half an hour, a pair of headlights came down the long path from the road. A fog had rolled in by then. This softened the beams and tinged them with yellow. I stood up and began waving at the same time, wondering whether or not this late-night motorist was Bethany. The car veered toward me and I felt a catch in my lungs, fear that I was alone in the dark.

"Charles!" Bethany yelled out the window. "Charles!"

She applied the brakes, making the car squeal and slide on

the gravelly asphalt. It was right out of an old movie, where the star-crossed lovers finally come together after war and famine and other cruel twists of fate.

A short black dress with no hose, lips a deep red, and every hair in place — that was Bethany.

"Baby," she said. And then she took me in her arms. "What's wrong?"

"I don't know," I said and it wasn't a lie. "I need to take a bath."

It only took ten minutes to get back to her place. She kept asking what had happened, what was wrong, but I said I couldn't talk yet. My teeth were chattering and I blamed the cold. She accepted my excuse. Maybe that really was why I couldn't talk.

"My roommate's gone back to Baltimore for the week," she told me as she gave me a big towel.

I spent a long time under the shower. I washed completely, even brushed my teeth with a blue brush I found on the sink.

When I came out, draped in the towel, I was ready to talk but the time for talking was over for a while.

We kissed more than I had kissed in my whole life. Long wet osculations with hungry little grunts punctuating our pleasure. I kissed her breasts and her toes, the round crack of her buttocks and spaces behind her thighs. I massaged her shoulders while licking the back of her neck. When she moved back to watch me, I kissed the blankets on her bed.

After we had made love, I held tight.

"Charles," she said. "Hold me."

The hugging went on into the morning. It led to many more bouts of passion. I was making up for a starvation diet, broken in a fit of fear.

The next day I asked Bethany to take me back to my car.

"When will I see you?" she asked.

"I don't know," I said. "I'll call you when all of this is over."

"All of what?"

"I don't know what, okay? I don't know."

She drove me without asking anything else. At the car she said, "Charles?" and hesitated. "Charles, I want to see you again."

"Me too," I said.

I left her feeling no shred of the love we'd shared the night before.

thirteen

After that night with Bethany, the days passed quickly. I spent most of the time reading sci-fi novels, but I unpacked the rest of Bennet's boxes too. There I found three tin plates, each broken into different-size segments like a TV-dinner tray, and a portable toilet unit that was to be connected by rubber tubing to a canister designed to empty the contents of the toilet. There was a box of books and various elastic exercising devices. A cigar box held three pens and two pencils with a dozen cream-colored envelopes along with a small ream of blank sheets of notepaper.

It seemed as if Anniston Bennet had everything he needed to live in that hole for a very long time.

The books were all hardback. *The Wealth of Nations*, *The Prince*, the complete collection of Will and Ariel Durant's *Story of Civilization*. Maybe ninety books in all. About fifteen of these were nonfiction (not including the Durants' eleven volumes), and most of these were economic texts and not titles that I knew. The fiction and poetry was of a high quality, for the most part. I recognized *The Alexandria Quartet* by Durrell and *The Adventures of Huckleberry*

Finn. He had the collected works of the poet Philip Larkin and *Four Quartets* by T. S. Eliot. *Moby Dick* was there and a book called *Vineland.* He also had the Bible and Koran. He had one very large atlas that didn't have any publication information in it. I got the feeling that it was privately published and contained specialized geographic information. Many of the maps were color coded with initials that made no sense to me and were not explained in any table.

They were all books that I would've liked to have read at some time in the past. I mean that I would've liked to know what was in the Bible and the history of the world so when I had arguments with Clarance I could sound smart. But I can't concentrate on that kind of reading. My mind just drifts when there are too many facts or tough sentences on the page. That's one of the reasons why I finally left college. As long as classes were lectures, I picked up most of what I needed by ear. But as soon as I had to read some heavy text, I was in deep water.

There were two sets of powder-blue pajamas decorated by red dashes at all angles to one another. All in all it was like a summer camp for a cracked adult.

All except for that cage.

Three days before Anniston Bennet was due to arrive, I received a telegram. It had been slipped under my front door sometime the day before.

Mr. Blakey,
After numerous attempts to reach you by telephone, we are contacting you by this method to confirm the appointment and to ask you to meet the client's train at 12:04 a.m. Please confirm your agreement by calling the number on the card that the client gave you at your first meeting.

There was no signature, but of course none was necessary. I thought the secrecy was strange, but then again Bethany had told me about rich people and how odd they were.

It took me the entire day to find that card. I turned the house inside out. Finally I found it in the upstairs hamper, in the pocket I had put it in after calling Bennet the first time.

"Hello," said a familiar voice. "You have reached the Tanenbaum and Ross Investment Strategies Group" — the click —"Mr. Bennet" —the next click —"is not in at the moment but will return your message at the earliest possible time. Please leave your name and number after the signal."

"I'll be there at midnight," I said and hung up.

And I was there, in the lamp-lit parking lot, at midnight. An obese family — the Benoits, mother and children — was also there, waiting. The Benoit family had come down to the Harbor from Montreal at the turn of the century. I don't remember ever having spoken to Raoul, the father, or any of his clan, but I knew them because they were part of my community. Trudy, the mother, looked at me nervously, a black man at midnight and the train not in yet.

"Hello, Mrs. Benoit," I hailed. "You meeting Raoul?"

I said it to put her at ease. It worked too. She smiled and nodded. She didn't remember my name. Maybe she couldn't distinguish between black men. But it didn't matter what white people saw when they looked at me. Why would I care?

The train came in and a few people got off. Most of them got into cars. Three taxis rolled up from the colored company that Clarance dispatched for. The few travelers who did not have cars climbed into the cabs. Raoul Benoit, a thin and dapper man wearing a silver-gray suit, tried to get his arms around his wife and failed. He kissed his children and herded them, like so many beach balls, toward a blue station wagon.

"Hey, Charles," a man said. Behind me Clarance had driven up in a cab. In the back there were three passengers, and another, a woman, sat beside my childhood friend. All of the passengers were white. The riders looked uncomfortable. One man in the backseat checked his watch.

"You drivin' now?" I asked.

"Athalia needs braces, so I'm drivin' three nights a week. How you doin'?"

"Fine," I said, looking over my shoulder.

"You need a ride?"

"No."

"What you doin' out here?" he asked. "Meetin' somebody?"

"Can we get going, driver?" the woman next to Clarance asked, barely restraining her impatience.

"Must be the next train," I said vaguely.

"Next train's tomorrow," Clarance informed me.

"Oh."

"Driver," a man in the backseat said.

"What?" Clarance's tone was sharp.

In the darkness, on the platform next to the station sign, I saw the silhouette of a small man.

"We need to get home," the passenger was saying.

"Well if you can't wait a minute while I find out how my friend is, then you could walk." That brought silence.

"You go on, Clarance," I said. "I got my car. I can drive home."

"I tried to call you," Clarance said.

"I been thinkin'," I replied.

"You wanna get together?"

"I'll call you next week," I said.

Clarance looked at me a moment. There was concern in his

face. He was a good man, and we had been friends as long as either one of us could remember. But there was no way to talk to me. He shrugged.

"See ya," he said and then drove off.

As he left, Anniston Bennet approached from the platform. I stood my ground, waiting.

"Good evening," he said.

The air was cool but my windbreaker was enough to keep the chill off. There were moths floating around the floodlights, and I detected the barely distinguishable motion of bats feasting on the fluttering bugs in the hovering darkness.

I took a deep breath and prepared myself. I wanted to start this thing with Bennet on the right foot. I never had a tenant before and didn't want to be taken advantage of. Everything mattered. The fact that I waited for him to walk to me, that I didn't offer to take his satchel. All he carried was that small leather bag. I wondered what he was planning to wear for two months.

"Mr. Blakey," he said.

"Mr. Bennet."

"I tried to call," he said. "But there was no answer."

"I know. I got the telegram. Did you get my message?"

He shrugged his shoulders, indicating that he was there because he received my message. That would have been a good moment for me to take his bag, but I did not.

"My car is over there." I indicated the brown Dodge.

We made our way. Bennet threw his bag in the backseat and we were off.

"Why did you need me to pick you up?" I asked, turning onto the highway. "You know we didn't say anything about you paying for a limo service."

"I want to be circumspect about this retreat, Mr. Blakey. No one knows where I'm going. Part of the idea is that I am to be kept from everything in my world — completely. I don't want my car in your driveway or some driver who remembers where he dropped me off."

"That sounds illegal, Mr. Bennet. I don't want to be involved in anything that's against the law."

He looked at me and laughed silently. Then he said, "Not illegal. No. You see, in my world I'm pretty well known, and some people think that I'm important — for their money. I don't want anybody finding me. This time is my own."

Off the side of the highway, I spotted three deer, their luminescent eyes transfixed by my high beams. We sped past them. I thought that at least they were witnesses to our passage.

"What were you laughing about?" I asked.

"Ask me later." Bennet sat back in the passenger's seat, letting out a deep sigh. It could have been pleasure or the last breath of a dying man.

"Can you pull into your garage?" Bennet asked me as we drove up my gravel driveway. "I mean, if we're going to see this secrecy thing through, we might as well do it right."

I almost sneered, but then I remembered Miss Littleneck. She was probably sitting on her front porch, smoking a cigarette and spying on the night. I wasn't sure if I wanted the neighborhood to know about my tenant, so I opened the garage door and drove in. Bennet and I exited out the back door of the garage and down through the hatch to the cellar. I snapped on the light and immediately Bennet began to inspect my work. I had unpacked and constructed a small red plastic table and chair. These seemed to satisfy him. There was also a futon that I had unfurled.

"Help me with these," he said, dragging the table and chair toward the small door of the cage.

He crawled into the cage, and with a little effort, I passed the furniture in to him.

He arranged the pieces like a small bedroom. I handed him the clothes and stationery and a few other small items.

"Pass the crapper," he then said. I dragged the oval-shaped cylinder to the door, and he strained over it until it was against the back wall of the cage.

"Now all we need is to put the pump back here and we're in business," he said.

He stood up then and approached me. Looking at him through the diamonds of the cage, I thought not for the first time that the structure might bear more than a resemblance to a prison cell.

"Have you figured it out yet?" he asked me as if reading my mind.

"What?"

Again the silent laugh.

"What?" I asked again.

"This is my prison," he said. "And you are my warden and my guard."

"Are you crazy?" The sentence just came out of my mouth. It wasn't really a question.

"You like to drink, don't you, Charles?" he asked. "Why don't you go up to the house and get us some liquor? I'll explain to you why I'm not crazy and why this is important for both of us."

It was a request bordering on a gentle command. There was no polite answer except to go get a bottle and two glasses. I wanted to be out of his presence for a minute. Anniston Bennet was a man who made you do what he wanted. He seemed reasonable and generous and know-ledgeable — not mad. But what he was saying made me want to run.

I walked away instead. Up toward the house and the cheap bottles of whiskey in the pantry, where I first heard Bethany's cries of passion and where my parents murmured deep secrets that made me feel at ease.

fourteen

"Let's just say..." Anniston Bennet was saying. I had brought my cheap whiskey and two squat glasses that had been on the shelf since before my mother could remember. I was sitting on the stairs and he had pulled out his red chair to join me. "...that I'm a criminal wishing to pay for my crimes."

"I don't get it," I said. "Why don't you just turn yourself in to the police if you want to go to jail?"

"I don't recognize any organized form of law enforcement, or government for that matter, as valid," he stated simply. He might have been a prime minister or anarchist. He could have even been some advanced form of alien life, looking down on humanity as we might look on a mob of ants. "But even if I did, there is no crime that I could be tried for in this country. Well, maybe some laws having to do with money. But I would never allow the hypocrites on our benches to stand judgment over me."

"I still don't get it," I said, downing my glass in frustration and refilling it with the gratitude of a full bottle. "What does my basement have to do with all that? What do I have to do with it?"

"Everything about us is random," Bennet said. "Maybe the universe has laws, but they aren't concerned about you or me or the people we touch. We're just mistakes who got up and walked off. The only things that are certain are death and the will to survive..."

He was a tiny man talking as if he were a giant. But he was convincing too.

"...We make our own victories and our own mistakes," he said, and for a moment there was a sad little chink in his armor of certainty. "There is no justice unless the judged agree. Without understanding and repentance there can only be revenge." He reached over to the stair next to me and refilled both our glasses.

"What are you talking about, Mr. Bennet? What kind of crime and justice and revenge do you mean?"

"The worst," he said. "You think of the worst crime you can imagine and then make it worse. And then you will have a glimmer of what I have done."

The whiskey was having an effect on both of us. My vision was skewed and the tone in his voice tended toward humanity.

"I don't need to know this," I said. "I don't need to be a part of it."

"But I paid you."

"To rent my basement, not to start a private prison. Damn, man. I don't know you. The police could come down here and find you all locked up. They could get me on kidnapping and who knows what else? No. No."

"Have you spent my money?" Bennet asked.

"I'll give you back what I have and then repay the rest."

"You need money, Charles. Why not take it when you can?"

"What do you know about me? What do you know about what I need?"

"Everything." He smiled and nodded.

"Like what?"

"I know where you went to high school and who your friends were. Clarance and Ricky, who you also call Cat. I know that you worked at Harbor Savings and that you embezzled four hundred and thirty dollars from your drawer..."

Whiskey softened the blow. I wondered if it was part of Bennet's plan to get me drunk.

"...The bank president, who liked you at first, felt betrayed, and blacklisted you among the town business community. Your mother and father are dead and no one else in your family is much interested in your well-being. You drink too much and you cried for five days after your mother's death. You had three years at Long Island City College. But you dropped out, didn't you? I don't know why you left. You had passing grades." Bennet peered at me with a Milquetoast expression on his face. "You're broke, you don't have a job, and there's a thirty-thousand-dollar mortgage hanging over your head that might lose your line their home."

"Where the hell did you get all that?"

"There's a man who used to work for me, a Filo Nunn. He now has a job for the investigation division of Morganthau and Haup."

"Who's that?"

"You wouldn't know, Charlie, but the bank president did. He started stuttering when Nunn got on the line. He understood that even the smallest toehold with that firm would completely transform his career in finance."

Bennet refilled my glass. I didn't even know that it was empty.

"So this guy, Nunn, found all that out? But you said that he doesn't even work for you anymore."

"Filo Nunn owes me his life." Anniston Bennet smiled again. If he had been a child, I would have said that he thought he was cute.

"I'm sorry, Mr. Bennet, but I can't go along with this. No. I will not be a part of this."

"That's final?" Bennet asked.

I nodded.

"But what if I made you a deal? What if I gave you the twenty-five thousand dollars now and we went ahead as we'd planned? Then in two weeks you tell me what you think. If the answer is still no, then I'll leave. If it's not I stay the rest of the time and double the final payment. All in cash. Always in cash."

I don't think the money interested me even that far back. And I was worried that once Bennet dug in, he'd be hard to dislodge. I was drunk but not that drunk. I remember the night and every word that was spoken. Maybe the whiskey made me less fearful. The consequences that bothered me earlier (and the next morning, for that matter) seemed manageable.

But that's not why I agreed to Bennet's request.

I agreed because of knowledge and intimacy. Anniston Bennet knew more about me than any other person — and he was still willing to enter this business deal. Those shocking blue eyes looked right into mine and knew what they were seeing. Not like Bethany and not like Clarance. Unlike Uncle Brent, Bennet made no judgments. If he felt he was better than me, it was only because he felt better than everyone, and that, in some strange whiskey-soaked way, made me an equal in the world — at least in the world as seen through his eyes.

"Yeah, all right," I said. "Let's do this thing."

Bennet smiled and retrieved the satchel from the floor next to his cell. He took five bound stacks of twenty-dollar bills.

"Twenty-five thousand, as we agreed," he said.

Then he came out with an ugly chunk of black metal that had some mechanical purpose that was not immediately obvious.

"It's an original lock used to hold down a line of slaves in the old slaving ships," Bennet told me. Along with the lock there was a brass key with a cylindrical tip that had teeth and slats made to fit the archaic mechanism. "It's over a hundred and fifty years old. I got it in Mali."

As far as I knew there was no one in the Blakey family who had ever been a slave. We came over as indentured servants and sailors on Spanish and Portuguese ships. It was even intimated that one distant cousin was himself a slaver, selling black bodies on the wharves of New York City from a ship called the *Dahomey*.

Many of my relatives didn't like to think that they were a part of the mass of blacks in this country. They would say, secretly, that they were no different from the English or Irish immigrants. But most Negroes, even the old families that dotted our neighborhood, understood that racism doesn't ask for a pedigree. I knew that many white people didn't like me because of my dark skin. I wasn't stupid. At the same time I didn't feel the pang or tug of identity when slavery was mentioned.

But that lock was a vicious thing. It must have weighed four pounds. The loop of metal used to secure the bolt was half an inch thick. I could imagine that ugly device holding down twenty men in the cold fastness of the Atlantic.

Bennet worked the key, which was new, in the lock and the long loop came away from the barrel-like body.

"It fits the center hinge on the door," he said.

He crawled into the cage, dragging his red chair, and I fit the lock through and slammed it shut. Then I pulled hard to make sure that the lock held.

The loud crack of the lock snapping shut had a pronounced effect on my self-proclaimed prisoner. His face visibly paled and he grabbed onto the bars of the door with both hands.

"I thought you wanted this," I said.

"I do."

"Then why do you look so scared?"

"I had certain experiences thirty years ago that made me nervous about close spaces and locked doors," he said.

"So then why you want to lock yourself in a basement?"

"This is a punishment, Mr. Blakey, not a vacation."

fifteen

After I'd locked him in, I brought my prisoner some water and a dry ham-salad sandwich that I made from white bread and a can off the shelf. There was a small space between the bottom of the cell door and the floor. This space was large enough to pass the tin plate and squat glass through.

"Lights out," I said at the hatch.

The look in his eyes was both frightened and resolved.

I pulled the string on the lightbulb. I decided to put a lock on the hatch door in the morning. For one night in the hole, he could go without security.

I didn't sleep much that night. Fidgety and nervous, I broke out into sweats every now and then. Sounds that could have been the hatch to the basement drove me from the bed a half-dozen times. I looked out the window and once even ventured into the yard. I didn't lift the cellar door though. I didn't want to show Bennet how scared I was.

He was locked up in a nine-foot cell and I was still afraid of him. Actually the fear started when the lock engaged. He was empowered by the fact of his helplessness. And I was at risk. I lay in bed worrying about kids sneaking into the cellar and finding Bennet. Then they'd tell their parents and then the police would come...

One of the few times I fell off to sleep, I dreamed that I was in a courtroom. Lainie and Mr. Gurgel and Ira Minder testified that I was a bank robber. They said that it was armed robbery because I had carried my pocketknife to work and, somehow, the pocketknife turned into the .22 rifle that was in a box on the shelf in my father's library. The judge found me guilty. I was convicted, sentenced, and put into Bennet's cell. But it was much smaller than nine by nine, more like three by three. I couldn't stand up and there was barely any light. A wave of despair so profound went through me that I was standing next to the bed before I came awake. I wanted to run. I wanted to cry. I definitely wanted Anniston Bennet out of my life.

I roamed the rooms of the house after that, going from floor to floor trying to figure out how I could beat this thing. I wanted a drink but my stomach and intestines were roiling. I couldn't even make out words in the books I paged through.

I was up in the old fortress, my mother's sewing room, when the sun hit my great-grandfather's old oaks. Amber, orange, a hint of yellow, and deep-blue strips made the horizon line. They were the colors of majesty's approach. I was arrested by the promise of morning light. I imagined those deer I had seen all dewy and shivering in the morning chill. The night was behind them, and if the air smelled clean and clear of danger, they marked another night gone with hunger and thirst for the next.

I awoke with my head on a bag of pieces my mother kept for quilting. The sun was hot on my ear and my own loud breath was like a wind tunnel.

Outside the granite headstones stood in the high weeds like soldiers hunkering down in the grass before a morning assault. My mother spoke to me then. "You should cut those weeds," she said as clearly as if she were still alive. It was the first time I had ever imagined hearing her voice.

"Yes, ma'am," I said.

I showered and shaved, brushed and ironed. Anniston Bennet's breakfast — a boiled egg, cornflakes, and apple juice — was ready at 9:23.

When I opened the hatch, a scent assailed me. It wasn't strong but it was living — the man in my basement taking ownership with his spoor.

"Good morning, Charlie," Bennet said as I stooped over to slide the tray and glass under the cage door.

"The name is Charles Dodd-Blakey. You can call me Mr. Dodd-Blakey, Mr. Bennet. That will keep us civil over the next two weeks." It was a voice I hadn't heard in many years — fourteen years. The tone I used on Uncle Brent when he was lying in his bed dying, smelling up my home with death.

Bennet's thin eyebrows raised. He took up the tray and stood, using his toe to push the previous night's tray out. I realized that I was expected to take his dirty dishes and wash them — like a manservant, a butler doing his master's dirty work for him.

"Okay." He paused. "Mr. Dodd-Blakey. Good morning to you. Did you sleep well?"

"I'll connect a hose from the sink that you can use to wash your dishes," I replied. "It's just cold water but that'll have to do. You want me to leave the light on?"

"I didn't get my books last night," he said. "Would you get them for me?"

"Which one did you want?"

This curt question caught Bennet up short. He put out a hand and touched the metal slats of his cage. For a moment hardness shone in his eyes, but then he said, "The first volume in the *Story of Civilization*."

I complied without comment. The book was a tight fit under the cage door and the cover ripped.

"Maybe you could open the door for the other ones," Bennet suggested.

"The only reason that lock comes off," I said, "is when you get your ass out of here."

"You sound angry, Mr. Dodd-Blakey."

I regretted having asked him to refer to me in that way. It was a show of respect, but not to me. I was Charles, son of Mr. Blakey.

"Not angry," I said. "It's just... just this whole thing is weird."

"What?" Anniston Bennet asked, sitting back in his chair behind metal bars as if he were in his den in Greenwich.

"You," I said, "in this cell under lock and key, with me like some kinda warden and butler all rolled up into one."

Bennet smiled.

"Have you ever read the *Story of Civilization*?" he asked.

"A long time ago," I lied. "I'm not so good on a lotta details though."

"All throughout history there have been men who have isolated themselves from the world," he said. "They go to mountaintops or sit in meditation for months at a time. They flagellate themselves and refrain from having sex or masturbation. That's mostly what I'm doing here."

"But you said that you're a criminal paying for his crimes," I pointed out.

Anniston Bennet smiled and hunched his shoulders as if to say, *You got me there*.

"Many ancient belief systems are based on the concept of sin, my friend," he said. "The Hindus accept as truth that they are answering for crimes committed in previous lives. The Hebrews and Christians are answering for the sins of their long-ago ancestors."

"But that's not you, is it?"

"No. I don't have the luxury of a god. But what I do have is not contagious."

"Come again?"

"In the eyes of the world, Mr. Dodd-Blakey, I am an upright and innocent man. My time here with you would be seen merely as an eccentricity. You can collect my money and serve me dry sandwiches and Kool-Aid. No one will blame you or indict you for the crimes that I recognize as my own."

"That's just a lot of talk, Mr. Bennet. I think that it's crazy what you're doing, but I took your money, so I'll hold up my side of the bargain. But don't you think that I'm gonna be a part of all this crazy talk. I'll bring you your meals and whatever else I have to do. But I don't like it and I'll put you out of here in a minute if anything gets to be too much for me."

I don't know how he felt about that because I left before he could engage me anymore. Outside the cellar I began to sweat. My heart was pounding and my ears rang. Inside my chest there was laughter, but the mirth could not make its way to my lips. It came as a throbbing rumble that might have been pleasant if it had an outlet.

I stumbled to the house, up to my room. There I sat on the old maple bed, thinking about Brent and all the mean things he had said to me. I imagined him walking down the halls in his slow shuffling pace. I thought about him cursing the summer for its heat and the winter for cold. I hated his smell and scratchy voice.

I could almost hear him, his wheezing through those last dying days.

Ears ringing, heart pumping, chest throbbing, and sweat dripping, I tried to rise above my body, hoped for my spirit to transcend grief.

It was grief I felt. Deep sadness that no mother or god could calm. I hated Anniston Bennet, hated him. I blamed him for everything that was wrong with me. His damned money and smirks.

I was wondering how long a boiled egg and cornflakes could keep someone alive. Everything was orange colored through closed lids, and my skin was dry and cool.

I opened my eyes. The air and the light in the room told me that it was afternoon. I had been dreaming of the prisoner's luncheon. His life was like an invisible pulsing beacon, second heart, a child who needed attention. He was living in my dreams as well as my cellar. I despised him already and he hadn't even been there a whole day.

I prepared baked beans from the can, boiled potatoes, and cranberry juice for his late lunch. He was already halfway through the thousand-page volume of history, wearing red-rimmed glasses and sitting in the red plastic chair. The breakfast tray was already pushed out. I shoved the lunch tray into his cell.

"What time is it?" he asked.

"Four," I said, turning to leave.

"It's not so bad, is it?" he asked.

I turned back and said with false bravado, "Not bad for me at all. I'm not the one locked up in a cold basement on a summer day. I'm not the one kept away from my family and friends."

"That's true," he said. "But you know there's a belief that any society that is forced to punish its citizens is, to one degree or another, an unhealthy state."

"That's crazy," I said. "What country do you know of doesn't have laws?"

"It's a question of degree, Mr. Dodd-Blakey," Bennet replied, "not one of law. A man who recognizes his crime and accepts his punishment is a member of good standing in his country. But the criminal who runs and hides, who is unrepentant even though he knows what he's done, is a symptom of a much greater disease."

"None of that has anything to do with you being here," I said. "You're renting a room and locking the door — that's all."

"No," the enigmatic white man said to a space somewhere over my head. "I am here answering for crimes against humanity. I am doing so because I am guilty, not because I was caught. And in doing so I am making the world a better place. I'm setting an example down here."

"How can you be doing that when no one even knows where you are?"

"There's more to the world than one plus one, Mr. Dodd-Blakey."

I barely heard him over the pounding of my heart. I worried that maybe he wasn't crazy, that he wasn't even a common crook. Even though I didn't understand what he was saying, I feared that maybe he was right, that he was living out some moral dilemma and that I was caught up in the center of it all without knowing it.

Once outside I was sweating again. I didn't want to go in my house, so I got in the car and drove into town. I went to Harbor Savings with the money Narciss had sent. The teller went over the check for a full minute before cashing it. Everyone in the Harbor must have known about my thefts.

From the bank I went to Nelson's Hardware, where I bought three combination padlocks and heavy hinges to hold them. Ricky was sitting on a public bench on Main Street, drinking orange juice from a carton. I pretended not to notice him from across the street.

"Hey, Charles," he called.

I looked up, feigning surprise, and then crossed over to him.

"Hey, Cat," I said. "I thought you were working for Wilson Ryder?"

"Took the day off," he said. "Clarance said he saw you at the train station in the middle of the night."

"Yeah. I met some girl and she said she wanted to come back out to see me, said she'd be on that train but damned if she was." I lied smoothly and without a skip.

"Who is she?"

"Abby Peters," I said, pulling the name out of thin air.

"White girl?"

I said nothing then. If he wanted to wonder about something, I thought it would be best to have him thinking about a girl who didn't exist.

"Clarance said that you looked upset," Ricky said.

"Upset?"

"Well actually he said crazy. He said that you had a crazy look in your eye." Ricky cocked his head to the side in order to see up into my eyes. He was searching for insanity.

"How are you, Cat?"

He made a painful face. "Bethany dropped me."

"When?"

"Almost two months but I still miss her." The honest hurt in his voice and eyes told me that he had no suspicions about who Bethany was with now. "It hurts way down. You know, that girl could get somethin' cookin' in me. I was thinkin' about startin' some kinda serious business, about makin' a life for myself, for us. You know?"

"You always got life, Cat. Or else you don't have it. There is nothing else." It sounded right when I said it. Now it's just a meaningless line of words.

"*Are* you crazy, Charles?"

I laughed and said, "Just tired, Ricky. Tired of every day."

"What you mean?"

"I want something else, I guess. Something different."

"Like what? A vacation?"

"Maybe a journey," I said. The words were coming from my lips, but I wasn't thinking about them.

"What's the difference?" Ricky asked.

"A vacation's over after two weeks. You go out on a journey and you might not ever come back."

sixteen

That evening I took three suits from the hall closet. I hadn't worn a suit since I worked for the bank. There was a brown one, a deep green, and a blue so dark that I bought it thinking it was black. They were all cleaned and pressed. Before he got sick my father had repaneled all the closets with cedar, so no moths had gotten to them. I rummaged around for some dress shirts and ties. They were my father's, but we were the same size. His suits fit me too. They seemed to have more character than my straight-cuffed wear. His pants were roomier in the thighs. His socks were argyle. He had bigger shoulders than me, so the jackets were loose but stylish. There were a dozen of his suits in my mother's closet. And they covered the rainbow.

I'd always wondered why he had so many suits. He was a butcher in Southampton his whole life until he died. I guess he just liked them.

I brought Bennet a Big Mac and fries at about 9:00. He wanted to talk to me, but I didn't bite. I just shoved his food in and carried the dirty dishes back to the house.

*

The next day, after feeding the prisoner, I put on a white gabardine that my father wore and a dark-blue dress shirt and cream-colored tie. Tennis shoes were all I had to go with the ensemble, but they looked good in the full-length mirror. I noticed something different about me, but I wasn't sure what it was. It might have been the hipster clothes, but maybe it was something else.

Giving up that mystery, I drove off to see Narciss Gully.

She wasn't expecting me. The door to her shop was locked. But after a long while, she came from somewhere and peered through the linen curtains.

Seeing me, she was startled. I don't know if it was the suit or the surprise appearance, but she opened the door and said, "Mr. Blakey? What are you doing here?"

"Thought I'd check up on my business." The words didn't sound like me and the voice was queer. I didn't know why I had come out to Bridgehampton, to the little converted cottage that Narciss used as her shop and home.

You had to step down to enter the house. The front room was large and there were quilts everywhere — hanging from the walls, spread out on chairs, folded in stacks in the corner. The designs were rude on the whole and the cloth was old, stained, and often yellowing. The dominant color was white, and that made the room nearly glisten. Narciss wore a black skirt that came down to midcalf. It clung to her slender figure and stood out against the whiteness of the room. Her skin, with its subtle variations, seemed like a black-and-brown flame that had been stylized in a painting.

"I was working out back," she said as an excuse or maybe as a reason to be left alone.

"I thought this shop was your work?"

"It is — in a way. I'm writing a book too, about the Negro

quilts of the northeastern states. I hope that it will be a historical document as well as a craft and collecting resource. Harvard University Press wants to publish it." She rubbed her long fingers against the side of her face and looked down at the floor.

"That sounds nice," I said. "How long you been working on it?"

"Years," she said, smiling an apology.

"Good work needs time," my mother said often and I repeated then.

She smiled again and I blessed my mom.

"How's it going with my stuff?" I asked.

"Great. I've sent out all of my inquiries and people are starting to respond. A few serious collectors of African American art were interested in the masks, but I told them that they were in your permanent collection." She looked at me, and there was something like pride in her eyes.

"How much do you think we'll get in the end?"

"I don't know, maybe eighty thousand dollars."

If I was in my own clothes, speaking my own words, I would have probably yipped and shouted. Instead I stuck my lips out and nodded.

"That sounds good," I said. "Sounds like what I expected."

Narciss was happy to be appreciated. I was happy that she was happy.

"I've been reading about your masks," she said. "They're really interesting. They were used for tribal identification, but they also were to remind their owner of their home and family — their people."

I was listening close enough to have repeated her words but I wasn't concerned. Her skin and fingers and figure so slight that it seemed like they could be easily broken — that's what I was thinking about.

"You know I'm busy for the next couple of weeks," I said. "But maybe after that we could have that dinner we keep missing."

Miss Gully's mind was in Africa and history and identity, but I don't think she was upset to switch over to dating.

"That would be nice," she said. "You know, I've tried to call you a few times, but there's never been any answer."

"I've been away some lately."

"Oh? Where have you been?"

"Down to the city. I've been considering working in Manhattan for some time now. You know, I've been here my whole life. I think it's time for a change."

"Oh. But the city is so crowded, so overwhelming."

I laughed in a knowing way. "Sometimes I'm crowded and overwhelmed just living in my own head."

Who was it talking? Not me. At least I didn't think it was me. Whoever it was, Narciss seemed to like him. She smiled and pinched my baby finger with her forefinger and thumb.

I left there, making a beeline to Bethany's apartment.

She answered the door and we fell into each other's arms, not wasting a single word.

When our passions were satisfied, she lay against my chest and started crying.

"What's wrong?" I asked her.

"I wait for this every day," she sobbed. "I love you, Charles. But you don't care."

"There's a lot going on right now, honey. A lot that I can't talk about yet."

"You got a girlfriend?"

"No. Not that. It's inside my head. My head."

"Will you stay with me tonight?"

"I have to go."

"To her?"

"To who? I'm not going to anybody."

"If you aren't going to anyone, then why do you have to go? Don't you like being with me?"

"I can't explain it, Bethy," I said and then stood up from the bed. I still had a half-hard erection. Bethany stroked the hard-on lightly underneath and it jumped at her touch. But I put on my pants anyway, being careful not to do any damage to myself with the zipper.

"If you go now you can't come back," she said.

I didn't answer. I didn't really care.

She didn't follow me from the bedroom. Her roommate, Robin Talese, was sitting in the living-room chair. I wondered if the chubby white girl had listened to our hollering out love earlier on. From the way she was staring at my crotch, I was pretty sure that she had.

"Where have you been?" Anniston Bennet shouted when I returned to the cellar at about 10:00 that night.

"I had car trouble," I said. "Flat tire outside of Bridge-hampton. Sorry."

I handed him a Kentucky Fried Chicken four-piece meal that came with a biscuit, corn on the cob, coleslaw, and a root beer. The large paper cup wouldn't fit under the bars, so I creased it and poured the soda into a squat glass he'd used for lunch.

"You can't leave me down here all day without a meal," Anniston said in an angry but soft tone.

"You want out?" I asked. "You can leave anytime."

He didn't have an answer to that.

"You want the light to eat by?" I asked.

"Please," he said.

I left without sweating for the first time. And I slept the whole night through.

seventeen

The next ten days passed as one. Every day was the same as far as I was concerned. I delivered Bennet's meals at regular intervals. I pumped out his toilet twice and gave him books. I never spoke to him except to answer specific questions, and he was pretty quiet most of the time.

Sometimes I'd come into the room after he'd gone to the toilet. The smell was bad and I'd leave as soon as I could. The air was pretty dead in there, so I opened the hatch twice a day to freshen up the place with an electric fan.

For my part I dressed in my father's clothes and went down to Curry's, an East Hampton bar where tourists and summer residents went to mingle and get drunk. I met people there and joked around and drank beers. Not too much drinking. Just enough for a buzz. There were some nice white girls there who liked me, but I always went home alone.

I received two letters in that time. One was from Bethany apologizing for how angry she got at our last meeting. She understood, she said, that I was under stress and that we didn't have the kind of relationship where she could make demands. She hoped that I would understand how strongly she felt about me and that I would call soon. The words she used were different but that's what she said.

The other letter was actually a postcard. It was Narciss saying that she was looking forward to our dinner and asking when I would answer my phone.

I kept those letters on the windowsill next to my bed, beside the passport masks that I had standing there.

Many nights I would imagine some Senegalese or Congolese sailor on a Portuguese ship, carrying his mask to a new land. A black man, infinitely darker than me, with bright whites in his eyes, making his way to a world his people had never even imagined. And when he saw America, he jumped ship. The white people feared him as the devil, so he probably took on a Shinnecock bride. He came out to just about where I was now and built a life that most people never even suspected.

Between my make-believe ancestors and the women who loved my shadow, I was happy. Drinking and masturbating and feeding my prisoner three times a day. Wearing my father's clothes (sometimes even using his name) and pretending that I was a summering lawyer or stockbroker. Life meant nothing, but I was having a good time.

And then, two days before Anniston Bennet had agreed to leave, I went down to serve his dinner.

"Will you let me have a whiskey?" he asked mildly.

"Sure," I said. I was feeling flush and generous. Why not give the convict a snort?

I went to the house and returned with a bottle and a glass.

"I don't really want to drink alone," he said. "Here, you use the clean glass. I've got one from lunch."

I poured the whiskey for both of us and then sat on the large trunk used to deliver his books.

124

"It's pretty odd being locked up down here," he said. "It's great for reading. You can really concentrate if there's no phone or messages or radio. I mean, I don't even know what's gone on in the world for almost two weeks. But I know about the Renaissance as if it happened this morning."

He was the same man who came to my door two months before. Friendly and humble in his gestures. He didn't fool me this time, but I was fascinated by the show.

"Tell me, Mr. Bennet..."

"Yes, Mr. Dodd-Blakey?"

"Doesn't anybody miss you? Don't you have a mother or wife or good friend who you play golf with on Saturdays? Isn't somebody asking where you are?"

"Does anybody wonder about you, Mr. Dodd-Blakey?" His demeanor changed just that quickly. Suddenly he had an insight to my soul. My heart gave a quick gallop and I groped for an answer. But I needn't have worried.

"I mean," he continued, "we all disappear sometimes. We have to go to the toilet or sleep, go to work or down the street for some bread. It might take five minutes or ten. It might be overnight. Sometimes you forget to call or have to stay an extra day. Sometimes you fall in love with someone else or have an accident. One day you die."

He smiled knowingly, toasting me with his glass. I joined him in the drink and then poured the second round.

"One day you just don't come back," he said. "People are worried at first. They make calls to the police and hospitals. They hire detectives. They lose sleep. Some people are so close to their loved ones that they'd die without them. But most of us don't. Most of us adapt. We recognize thirst. We go to the toilet and close the door for privacy. We eat. New lovers and friends take the place of those we miss. People die every day,

Mr. Dodd-Blakey. We live in the valley of death. That's our heredity."

"But you aren't dead, Mr. Bennet. You're alive and locked up in a cage in a stranger's basement. You aren't in love or lost or the victim of some car crash or mugging. You're in a hole in the ground reading books and farting out cornflakes."

Bennet laughed. I poured two more drinks and relaxed. In the back of my mind I worried about letting my defenses down against this crazy white man, but then I thought to myself, *He's locked up; what can he do to me?*

"But I could be dead," he said. "Just like the man who goes away to prison, I'm gone from the lives of my peers. Anathema and death are the same thing. Most people don't want to go to prison or even to know about it. They don't want to go to the toilet with you or witness your fear. No one wants to watch you starve or bleed or suffer in any mortal way. We can't help but to see ourselves in one another, and what we want to see is beauty and life."

"You don't sound like a businessman, Mr. Bennet. You sound more like a philosophy teacher."

"I don't teach," he said. "But I'm not what you would call a businessman either. I'm a specialist."

"Yeah, yeah, I know, in reclamations."

"That's right." He smiled. "But the word has a different meaning than one might think."

"Like what?"

"Suppose," he said, "you knew that there were diamonds in the ground somewhere in Montana. Diamonds. Fabulous wealth. But worthless unless you could retrieve them. As worthless as dirt."

"Get a mining company going and dig," I said.

"But you're not quite sure where they're located. You have

the knowledge to go looking, but you don't know who owns the land. Maybe it's government land, maybe an Indian reservation. Maybe some old communist has it. You don't know."

"That's why they have corporations," I said. "You go into business with somebody and take your share."

"But you don't know who to go into business with. You don't know where the diamonds are, and if you let the word out, people will start looking on their own. If they have your knowledge, then they don't need you."

It made sense and I nodded. The whiskey tasted rich. I smacked my lips.

"No," Anniston Bennet said. "The diamonds only exist for the man who has imagined them. They only exist for the man who knows and who can realize their extraction. That's where I come in. Through various means I locate the wealth and then acquire the property that contains it. I'm paid handsomely for every step, and then I receive a stipend based upon the value of my reclamation."

"But it's not really something reclaimed," I argued. "It belonged to someone else and you took it. It's more like stealing."

"No," he said, shaking his head. "Knowledge is the only true prerequisite for ownership. If you don't know something, then you can't work with it. There are only two things that are important in ownership. The first, like I said, is knowledge. The second is the ability to exert control over the wealth. Seize the day. That's what I do."

"So you work in Montana?" I asked in a doubting tone.

He smiled at my insight. I was proud of his attention and embarrassed by my pride.

"No," he said. "America has been picked clean. There's no

wealth here. Not in its natural state, at any rate. There's no meat on the bone. I mean, I guess there's some potential. I've been playing with the idea of real estate and graveyards. That's one natural resource that could give up a few bucks."

I poured the glasses full. I drank and experienced a certain tipsy joy, but it wasn't just the liquor. I was in the presence, I believed, of a kind of mastermind, a Moriarty or Iago. A man who had been across the line of lies that defined good and evil for most normal folks. I mean, we all say at some time or other that politicians are crooks or that the rich are the best thieves. But no one seems to really know how they cheat and steal. It always comes as a surprise when some politician has taken money. As a matter of fact, it's hard to see sometimes when a crime has been committed even when it's been proven and documented. But Mr. Bennet could explain the arcane practices of the rich and powerful, and he was willing.

"So you spend your time making up schemes," I prompted. "Figuring out where to *reclaim* something nobody has found yet."

"No. Most resources are already known. There's uranium in some third-world countries. Other natural deposits or labor that's dirt cheap. The usual question is the cost of extraction. How much do I have to put in compared to what I can pull out? No. I don't have to find lost treasure. The companies come to me as a kind of consultant when they want to get in on the ground floor or, more often, when they want to keep a good thing." Bennet clasped his hands under his chin as if he were preparing to pray.

"It's a complex world, the one in which we live," he said. "The elements of power — greed, public opinion, applied wealth, hunger, the natural distrust between groups, and the quirks of politics and current events — must be dealt with in such a way that you and your tribe are able to end up on top. Sometimes it's simple. A million dollars in a military bag or toward both sides in a political campaign can yield hundreds of millions. You never have to worry about your commitment to a side or ideology. Your ideology is always the same. It's amazing," he said, looking up at me in wonder, "how a girl-child of eighteen can get a senator or prince to the conference table."

"Do you kill people too?" I asked. God bless whiskey, I say. Four shots and I knew no fear.

His look was both stern and startled. His left eye quivered; his shoulders hunched slightly.

"Life," he said, "has little to do with progress. More often than not men make the decisions that lead to their own deaths. They delegate, hate, stay when all the signs say go. Mostly they're unwilling to make a deal. And they're almost all forgotten. No better remembered than a cockroach who succumbs to a poison that you set down under the pantry six months before.

"Did you kill the Kurds in Iraq? Was Roosevelt guilty of the gassing of the Jews because he refused to bomb the camps or the rails leading to them? What about God at the River Jordan using Moses as his word?"

It was a good enough answer for me. Even leaning toward drunk, I didn't want the details.

"Yeah," I said. "I guess we all have some blood on our hands. If America does something, then the people do it too. That's why they call us Americans."

It was a lame attempt to end what my question had started. I believed every word that Anniston Bennet had said, and I didn't want to hear any more. He smiled, understanding my discomfort.

"Could you bring me down some detergent?" he asked. "I'd like to wash out my uniforms. They're starting to smell."

I went up to the house and brought back a cupful of soap flakes. I also brought a flatish and wide aluminum bowl that slid neatly under the locked cage door. He thanked me and I left quickly.

The moon was out that night, and I watched it for a long time. Well, I didn't watch as much as I looked. Because my mind was not on the moon but back in the basement, hearing things that were something like ancient secrets that had been revealed coincidentally in my presence.

eighteen

Up in my room, I studied the passport masks on the windowsill. I had them standing on their chins with their heads propped up against the glass. One's mouth formed an O, making him seem like he was singing. The two others were tight-lipped, maybe humming the music for their brother's song.

Maybe they were black slavers, I thought, and maybe Anniston Bennet's ancestor owned the ship that they navigated.

I realized that I wasn't afraid or upset for the first time in many years. And even though I had had a lot to drink, I wasn't tired or even tipsy anymore. The talk with Bennet exhilarated me. I didn't even remember at that time what he'd said. I just knew that it was important, that I was privy to a way of thinking that wasn't taught in schools or at the dinner table. In some crazy way it was what I liked about the wild. There were no moral laws or rules governing the lives of wolves and bears. Those creatures lived only by the instinct of survival. What Bennet said about the world was the same thing, only with the added ingredient of sly thought. Looking out of my window, I wanted to howl at the moon.

*

The night moved along, but I did not tire. Snatches of phrases kept returning from my discussion with Bennet. Knowledge and ownership, a hundred times the return on an investment. But most of all I was taken by his confidence and certainty. He *knew* how the world worked. Not like Clarance or the construction boss Wilson Ryder. They just repeated what they read in books or what they wanted to believe. I believed that Bennet knew the truth that lay under the newspaper stories and the hypocrisy of politics. He made me question what was, when for a whole lifetime up till that moment, I accepted the world's excuses.

Wandering the house and thinking about my prisoner, I was still awake at 2:00 in the morning. Not only awake but excited. All of my fears about being tricked and sent to prison —all of my worry about how odd Bennet was — dissipated with the thrill of a new way of seeing the world.

I tried to lie down, but sleep wouldn't come. Finally I decided to call Narciss. Not her, actually, but the answering machine at her store. I wanted to go out with her, to discuss passport masks and notions of power.

She answered on the first ring. "Hello?"

"Narciss?"

"Mr. Blakey? Is something wrong?"

"I'm sorry, Narciss. I thought that you wouldn't hear the shop phone. I was going to leave a message on your machine."

"It's okay," she said in a voice more sultry than usual. "I don't sleep very much. The doctor says it's my metabolism. I take naps during the day and work most nights."

"On your book?"

"On anything. I read and quilt and watch bad TV."

"Huh. I sleep most nights through. But tonight I was just up."

"What's wrong?"

"Nothing."

"Then why did you call?"

I wasn't prepared to set up a date with a real person. Not with Narciss at any rate.

"Did you ever study evil at college?" I asked instead. The question surprised me. "I mean, what people in the past thought made a man evil, bad?"

"No," she said with a note of wonder in her voice. "No, we never studied that. And now that you mention it, it seems that it should have been at least a seminar if not a whole branch of study."

"That's the thing, right?" I said. "I mean, here we got evil all over the place: in our history books and fiction and on movies and TV. We just fought a war against a supposedly evil man, but then if you ask what *evil* is, everybody has a different answer."

"I suppose they cover it in divinity school," Narciss said, "but that would be religious, and you're really asking about something else. The idea of evil. Why do you ask?"

Because I have the devil living in my basement — that's what came to my mind.

"I don't know," I said. "I was just sitting up thinking about it and I thought about you and archaeology and thought maybe you would know. I went to college for three years and I never heard anything about it."

"What college did you go to?"

"Long Island City College. I studied political science mainly."

"Why'd you stop going?"

"I don't know. I really don't. My grades weren't so good and I couldn't remember anything. Nothing. The last semester of my sophomore year I was going to fail a course in ancient political thought. Some of those guys talked about evil. But that was a long time ago. You'd think that there'd be a modern study of it."

"Are you ever planning to go back?"

"To school? No."

"Why not?"

"It doesn't mean anything to me. I mean, let's say I went back. I'd go for a year and a half and then I'd have a bachelor's degree. What then? They don't have political scientists in the want ads —"

"But they have jobs for college graduates."

I stopped myself before I could say any more. I realized that I was about to start talking like I always did. I was going to make fun of school and jobs and careers. That's what I always did when somebody tried to give me advice.

"I got other plans," I said. "School didn't do it for me and so now I have to find another way."

"What way?"

"Reclamations," I said. And then before she could ask another question — "It's a form of international finance. I've been studying with a guy named Dent. He's been, ah, tutoring me, kind of. That's one of the reasons I go down to New York. I meet with Mr. Dent every week or so."

"Is he a teacher?" she asked.

I could tell by the tone in her voice that she believed me. But that's not what shocked me. I was stunned that the lie, as it came out of my mouth, became truth. The most important part of what I said was true. I was Bennet's student. That's why I was wandering the house, because I was learning.

"Yes," I said to Narciss's question. It seemed like hours since she asked it. "And no. I mean, it's not like school. We just happened into each other at Curry's bar a while back. He explained to me that he worked for multi-national corporations, helping them to acquire wealth all over the world. I was interested and he said that not that many people showed real interest in what he did. He agreed to teach me, to tell me what he knows."

"It doesn't sound good," she said. "It sounds like what all those American businesses do when they go to other countries and exploit labor or just steal. They say that Nigeria is one of the richest African countries, but most of the people there live in poverty. They say that's because of the oil companies."

"That might be, Narciss," I said in earnest. "But standing on the outside quoting Engels and Marx isn't going to help. Sayin' *that's not fair* won't do anything either. What I want is to find out, to get in there and see for myself. Because you know they aren't going to stop doing what they're doing just because we whisper something against them at night on the phone. I mean, I put gas in my tank, don't I? That's what voting is to big business, you know. It's not a secret ballot; it's a purchase. If you buy from him, that's your vote of confidence."

I was making it up as I went, but it sounded right. It sounded true. Snatches of classroom dialogues and dime novels, even some things my uncle Brent had said, came together in a lie that was fast becoming my life.

"Being true doesn't make something right, you know," Narciss argued. "Some things are wrong. Just because you know how to get some slave labor doesn't make it okay."

"I know that," I said, more as a musical beat than any

conviction. "I know. But if your hands are clean and people are still dying, then how can you say that you did better than me?"

"I don't know," she said after a short pause. "But I don't want to talk about it anymore. I . . . I have to go."

"Okay. I'm sorry if I bothered you."

"No, you didn't. Goodbye."

"Bye."

At one time I would have been near despair at that kind of ending to a phone call. So few women ever seemed to show an interest in me that if I had one on the line I never wanted to let go. But that morning I wasn't worried about anything. I had discovered my calling. Or at least I had found a door.

It was like a fairy tale my mother used to read to me — *The Brownie's Gift*. A child was walking in the woods looking for his cat, Bootsie, who had run away. The boy searched and called and was very very sad when he came upon an iron door in a tree. There was a tiny slit in the door through which the boy could see a small elfin creature — called a brownie — who was locked up and every bit as sad as the child. They made an alliance, boy and elf, that one would help the other and they would both be happy ever after.

I don't remember the particulars, but the brownie was freed and Bootsie was found. I spent years after that searching my ancestral woods for a door in a tree or the ground. I believed that somewhere there was a beneficent genie who I could free in exchange for happiness for all times.

I had found that door after thirty years of searching. It was the hatch to my own basement, and the brownie was a white man who wanted to be caged. No matter the differences the main story was the same. I went to bed thinking that I'd never fall asleep. But after only a moment I was unconscious beneath the heads of my ancestors.

nineteen

"Good morning," the naked man said to me. The prisoner was standing in the middle of his cell, his pajamas hung neatly from the back of the cage. The concrete surrounding his cell was dark from the water he must have thrown there. "I washed both pair last night. I wasn't at all tired."

Anniston Bennet had a huge uncircumcised penis. It was the biggest one I had ever seen on a human male. It just hung down flaccid and heavy between his thighs.

"I was thinking about our talk," he said, seemingly unconscious of his nakedness or endowment. "I don't usually think about things much. Usually there's too much to get done. I've lived a pretty active life, you know. But you had me thinking last night. And to answer your question —"

"What question?"

"About killing —"

"I have to go, Mr. Bennet," I said. I put down the fried eggs and heated potato patties and pushed them under the door to his cage. I was rattled by his ease at being naked. He wasn't a powerfully built man, small except for that big dick. And there was a cascading series of cross-hatched scars down his right shoulder that was painful to see. His feet were tiny. Something about standing there conversing with the naked man was too much for me.

"I'll be back this afternoon," I said. "We could talk then."

"Where you going?"

"To see my friend. We said we'd get together today."

He wanted to keep on talking, but I had to get out of there. I rushed up the stairs and slammed the hatch shut. I threw the newly attached bolts and secured them with the padlocks and went straight to my car.

I never did figure out what it was exactly that drove me from the cellar that morning. I have what I always thought was a normal-size penis. I've never measured or anything, but it has the feel of average. The women I've known were never surprised, one way or the other, when my erection was finally exposed to them. And even when they whispered sweet compliments, it had to do with how hard it got rather than how deep it went. Some men, I knew, were better endowed. Bethany had told me that it was just this fact that kept her attached to Clarance for so long. There were stories about Clarance's sexual prowess, but I had seen him in the boys' gym and he didn't hold a candle to Anniston Bennet.

I'd never felt embarrassed or inferior before that morning. And it wasn't just Bennet's anatomy but also his ease at being naked. As a child I learned to be ashamed of exposing my genitals or buttocks. Some dresses that women wear today make me avert my eyes.

I was halfway to Clarance's house before I realized that I had not lied to Bennet. It was Tuesday. Clarance always took Tuesdays off and worked the lighter Sunday shift. I got there a little after 10:00. His oldest daughter, Athalia, was sitting on the front porch. She was a big girl, sixteen I believe, and a magnet for boys.

"Hi, Mr. Blakey!" she shouted. "Daddy's havin' breakfast."

Even that small piece of information was delivered across the lawn in an engaging manner. Athalia was what is known as a daddy's girl. She loved to see men happy. I've often thought that Clarance must have sold his soul at some East Hampton crossroads to be blessed in so many ways.

"How's summer school, Thalia?"

"They suspended me 'cause I had a dirty magazine," she said, her smile dimming for a moment.

"You in trouble?"

"Naw. Momma's mad but Daddy just laughed."

She was wearing loose shorts and a pink blouse that didn't make it down to her navel. She caught my eye and I thought about Anniston Bennet — about how he was as unashamed as a child.

"When can you go back?" I asked.

"I gotta go Friday. I don't see why I can't just have the whole week off." She was bothered, but nothing kept Athalia down for long. She gave me a big grin and opened the door for me. I went through the small ranch-style house toward the back. There was no one in the dining room. Through the window I could see big Clarance sitting down to a meal at his cast-iron patio table. He was wearing shorts like his daughter, with a strap undershirt and red thongs. The iron table and chair were painted lime green. Behind him was a child's rubber pool in the middle of the back lawn. Clarance's house was a small affair, built in the midfifties. His family had lived in the Harbor for at least a hundred years, but they came from slaves down in Georgia. He still had cousins in Atlanta.

He saw me through the window and waved a turkey drumstick at me.

Once outside I hailed him. "Hey, Clarance."

"Charles." He used his drumstick to point out an iron chair, which I dragged to the table.

"You want some food?" he asked me.

"No, thanks."

"You look like you could use somethin', man," he said. "You losin' weight?"

That was what was different about my image in the mirror.

"How are you, Clarance?"

"Can't complain. Athalia had a *Playgirl* magazine at school and they kicked her out. Can you imagine that? Here they had lawyers holding up the president's dick on TV every night and they wanna suspend a girl for buyin' a magazine off the rack."

"Sorry if I was rude when I saw you at the train station," I said.

That raised Clarance's eyebrows a notch. It might have been the first apology that I ever gave without being forced into it.

"That's okay," he said. "You okay?"

"Been thinkin'. Been thinkin'."

"About what?"

"I don't know, Clarance. I guess I'm wondering why I'm out here doin' what I do. You know, there's nothing to it."

"What you mean?"

"It's like I've been asleep my whole life," I said. "And even now it feels like I'm still asleep, or almost out. I wake up for a minute and then three days go by and I wake up again."

"You mean you been up in your bed all this time?"

"Naw, man. Not sleeping — sleepwalking. I wake up and I'm in a store buying pot roast. Or somebody's talking to me, I mean I'm in the middle of a conversation, and I don't even know what the person just said. I don't even know what we're talking about or how I even got there. You know?"

I could tell that Clarance was concerned because he stopped eating.

"Like you black out?" he asked.

"No. If I think about it, I remember, but it's hard to concentrate. It's like nothing is important enough to think about."

What I was saying to Clarance had always been true for me — my whole life. Not a single day went by that I wasn't lost in daydreams. Teachers talking at you, my mother or father telling me what was right or wrong. The reason I didn't watch TV was because I couldn't sit still for a movie or sitcom. Halfway through a war film I still wasn't sure which side was which. I could read books, fun books, and I could follow an animal through the woods for hours. A blaze in the fireplace could keep my attention for a whole night. But anybody telling me anything was just a waste of good breath, as my uncle Brent used to say.

"Maybe you drinkin' too much," Clarance said.

"Maybe."

"You want a job, Charles?"

"What kind of job?"

"Driving a taxi. I could hook you up there."

I looked at Clarance, feeling like I had just come awake again. His act of kindness felt like the gentle nudge my mother used to give me when I was too tired to get up the first time she called.

"I got money," I said.

"How'd you get that?"

"Cat introduced me to Narciss Gully. She has an antique business. She specializes in quilts, but she's helping me sell the stuff that was in my cellar. It's a lotta money."

"How much?"

"Enough for the mortgage and a couple'a years or so."

Clarence didn't have much money. He worked hard at the taxi business, and his wife, Mona, was a nurse at the hospital in Southampton. Their families had nothing to give them. They spent everything on their kids. And so when Clarence still had concern on his face for my dilemma, I understood that he was a real friend. We'd known each other for thirty-three years, my whole life, and that was the first moment that I knew he really cared for me.

"I got to go, Mr. Mayhew," I said.

"You just got here. Stay for a while. Maybe we could go pick up Cat after work and go to some bars."

"No," I said. "But thank you. Thank you. And I'm sorry if I ever made you mad, man. You know I was just jealous. See ya."

I stood up from the iron chair and walked out past the teenager on the front porch. I glanced at her and realized that she was thumbing through the naked photographs in the *Playgirl* magazine that got her suspended.

"Bye, Thalia."

"Bye, Mr. Blakey. You come on back, okay?"

twenty

Bennet was dressed when I returned. Seated in the red chair, he wasn't reading or doing anything else as far as I could see.

"Mr. Dodd-Blakey," he said in greeting.

"Mr. Bennet," I replied.

It was an acknowledgment, the beginning of an understanding.

I pulled the trunk up to his cell and sat.

"What do you want?" I asked.

"To serve out my time. To pay my debt."

"Pay who?"

"Every minute I'm in here costs me something, Charles. May I call you Charles?"

"It's my name," I said.

"My business relations are delicate, Charles. My attention is needed sometimes within moments of certain events. When my phone rings I'm supposed to answer. If I fail to respond there are consequences."

"What kind of consequences?"

"That depends on the event." He shrugged and crossed one leg over the other. "Money might be lost, a political player could be discredited. Someone might die." He looked up at the ceiling. "Later on I'll be held responsible."

"By the law?"

"By the rules."

"Are the rules different than the law?"

He smiled in that knowing way. "The rules don't need a judge's interpretation. There's no defense. When you're absent you're dealt out. And then no one recognizes you but your enemies."

"All that's going to happen, but you still want to stay in here?"

"No." His impossible eyes looked straight into mine.

"Then why?"

"Have you ever been in love?" was his reply.

I stalled, not wanting to. I would have liked to have said *Of course. Everybody's been in love*. But it wasn't true. It wasn't true and I didn't want to lie to my new mentor.

I'd never been in love. Never even for a moment. I adored, idolized, lusted after, and cared for many women. I dated, kissed, had sex with; I waited for, stood by, and wanted. But I'd never been like those deer that moved together through the woods, keeping each other company as a matter of course. I'd never been attached by the sense of smell and warmth and security. I once read in a novel that love and gravity are the same thing, that natural attraction in nature is also the passion of man. I thought then that I was like a weightless astronaut, locked in a protective shell and floating in emptiness.

"Me neither," Anniston Bennet said, addressing my silence. "I've always done what I wanted to do or what I believed I needed. But I've never been brought to an action because of my heart."

It was almost ludicrous, listening to the *reclamations expert*'s talk about the heart, but I was moved anyway. The contradiction of emotions rattled around in my head.

"What's that got to do with you sitting down here locked up in a cage?"

"That's why I asked if you had ever been in love, Charles. Because love isn't a short skirt and shapely legs. It's not a clap of thunder or a chance meeting with a prostitute in a library in Paris."

"How would you know what it isn't if you've never been there yourself?" I felt dizzy and precarious on my trunk.

"I've never felt love, but I've studied it," he said. "In my line of work you pay attention to every human emotion the way doctors examine their patients. The desperation borne from hunger, for instance, is a powerful force that will turn the victim in on himself. It's the desire to devour the source of the pain. The pang of nationalism can make a man as blind and dense as a stone. He will cut off his own arm, kill his children, for a flag and a ten-cent song."

"But what about love?" I really wanted to know.

"Love, as the poet says, is like the spring. It grows on you and seduces you slowly and gently, but it holds tight like the roots of a tree. You don't know until you're ready to go that you can't move, that you would have to mutilate yourself in order to be free. That's the feeling. It doesn't last, at least it doesn't have to. But it holds on like a steel claw in your chest. Even if the tree dies, the roots cling to you. I've seen men and women give up everything for love that once was."

"And so you love somebody?" I asked. "That's what brought you here?"

"No," he said. "I don't have that affliction. I'm here alone and there's no one waiting or gone."

"So then why are you talking about love then?"

"Because that's the closest thing to what forced me into this cage. Everything else is immediate and measurable, pretty much. Fear, desperation, greed. I'm fifty-six years old, Charles. My first job was as an accountant in Saigon at the age of twenty-one. From there, on a forged Swiss passport, I got a job doing the same work for higher pay in Hanoi. My employers worried after accepting me that I was a spy. In order to test my loyalty, they brought me to a holding cell where there was an American sergeant held captive. They told me to kill him. They said that he had been sentenced to death anyway and that this was my first duty. And I shot him. I didn't hesitate or flinch. I didn't enjoy it or feel remorse. I just shot him."

"Killed him?"

"Scared the shit out of the officer who brought me down there. He expected me to balk. But I took the pistol and shot the man in the head. I saw the lay of the board immediately. The man had been tortured. He was skinny and bloody and miserable. They would have killed him anyway."

"Was it a black man?" I asked, wondering at the words even as I spoke them.

"I don't know" was his reply.

"How can you not know?"

"It was a dark cell and he was filthy. His skin wasn't black, but whether it was tanned or negroid I don't know. I didn't spend any time wondering about him. I took the pistol and shot. Then I left. The next seven years I worked back and forth across the borders of Communism and the West. That's where I made my nest egg. I had two million dollars by the time I came back home. On top of that I had connections with millionaires, intelligence agencies, and political leaders.

I even had a code name. They called me Sergeant Bilko because of my bald head and the fact that I could procure almost anything."

"Are they after you?"

"Who?"

"The Americans. I mean, you were a traitor."

"They don't care about that. They dealt with me too. I got three prisoners out from captivity for a fee. Asian communists are far more practical than the European variety."

"You still haven't explained why you want to be here."

"I don't want to be here, Charles. I have to be."

"Because you shot that man?"

"No. I mean, that's part of it. A small part. I've done a lot of things. Too many things. Sometimes it was that I did nothing. And now it's too late. Like with love, it's grown up all around me and I can't get away."

Again there was a break in Bennet's armor. He became distant and misty. Not near tears but vulnerable.

"And you think being down here will help make up for it," I said.

"No."

Through the diamonds of his cell Bennet took on the quality of a martyr. He was like one of those death-row inmates that they interview just before the sentence is executed. You see all the evil that they caused, but you still feel like death is not the answer — that killing this man would in some strange way take away his victims' last hope.

But Bennet wasn't going to die. He was on vacation. He was in the Hamptons for the summer. He was a thief and a murderer taking time off from his trade. This made me angry.

I began to resent the arrogance of Bennet. How dare he think that by pretending to punish himself that he would somehow have answered for his crimes.

"Why here, Mr. Bennet? Why my house?"

"There's lots of reclamations in Africa, Charles. Diamonds and oil, slave labor to cobble tennis shoes and assemble fancy lamps. They have armies over there who will strip down to the waist and go hand to hand with bayonets and clubs. They have tribal factions and colonizers. The streets, in short, are paved with gold."

"My house isn't in Africa."

"But you are a black man. You come from over there. I need a black face to look in on me. No white man has the right."

"Suppose I was crazy? Suppose I hated white people and I decided to torture you in here and kill you?"

He shrugged again. "Killing is hard work, Charles. Children have the stamina for that kind of labor, but most mature men do not. Not unless there's something to gain — or if they're in love."

"You're supposed to leave here in two days," I said.

"Unless you change your mind."

"Is this some kind of trick?" I asked. "Are you playing some kind of game on me?"

"No. I'm not, Charles. I'm simply executing a punishment. A repentance."

"You don't seem to be suffering to me."

"You wouldn't know," he said. "But living locked up with no out, with no control over food. Most of the time you won't even talk to me. And the world I live in is moving on while I sleep. No one knows where I am. When I get out of here, it's going to be hard on me."

In a flash of intuition I asked, "Is somebody after you now, Mr. Bennet?"

He was struck and smiled to show it.

"No more than they're looking for diamonds in Montana."

He laughed.

I laughed too.

"So you're a reclamation?" I asked.

"Can I have *The Alexandria Quartet*?" was his response.

"No. Tonight it's lights out and no book. Tonight you start your sentence for real and then we'll see how much you really want to be here."

A spasm twisted Bennet's face for half a moment. Hardly long enough for me to be sure of it. But I believed my sudden assertiveness frightened the smug assassin. I knew that he was afraid of the locked door and the dark.

twenty-one

That night I dreamed that there were agents of some malevolent power prowling around on my porch. I woke up at 3:00 a.m. wondering if I had really heard something. I found an envelope lying just outside the front door.

"She was here about five minutes ago," a voice said.

I yelped and jumped like a frightened eight-year-old.

Irene Littleneck was standing at the foot of the stairs, grinning at my little-girl shriek.

"I came over to see if she did something, but it was just a letter so I was going back. Then you come blunderin' down."

"It was a woman?"

"The one that came and moved all that stuff outta your house with that Puerto Rican boy."

"You were sitting outside?" I asked. It felt nice to have words with a neighbor even if it was 3:00 in the morning and I was running a private prison in my home.

"Havin' a cigarette," she said. "You know Chastity's too sick for me to smoke in the house. Doctor said that her lungs are too weak."

Irene had always been old. When I was five, she was in her

fifties. She and her sister, Chastity, used to come over and visit with my mother and Brent. I think Irene was sweet on my sour uncle.

"Oh," I said. "How is your sister, Miss Littleneck?"

"Not so good, Charles. She's been in that bed for almost a year now. I make her walk around the room twice a day, but it's getting harder and harder to get her up."

The sadness in Irene's voice was pitiful. She and Chastity had lived together their entire lives. But the only time I ever saw Chastity in the previous five years was when the ambulance came now and then to take her off to the hospital for some kind of treatment.

"I'm sorry to hear it, Miss Littleneck. If you need anything, just come over and ask, okay? If I'm not here just leave me a note."

"Oh, thank you, Charles. Thank you. Thank you." She was too far away to touch me, but she held out a thin hand anyway. Her gratitude was beyond anything I had said or done.

"Well," I said. "I better be getting back to bed. Goodnight."

"Goodnight," she said, but she didn't move until I went back inside my door.

Dear Mr. Blakey,

I apologize for getting off the phone so abruptly the other night. I called back the next day, but there was no answer. Tonight I was up late working on my book and I decided to write you.

I'm sorry for not giving you a chance to express your feelings about your business. I suppose that we're just of different temperaments and shouldn't try to force communication. But I want you to know that I do respect your wishes and I will execute the sale of your property with the utmost professionalism.

Sincerely,

Narciss Gully

The only reason I mention the letter here is to document how much my life had changed. Not my life exactly but the circumstances of my world. Narciss wanted me to call her, that is what I believed. She was up in the middle of the night thinking about me, trying to get me out of her head and then trying to write me out of, or into, her life.

All that and I was no closer to love.

I made coffee and plans instead of going to bed. I wanted something. I didn't know exactly what that something was, but I was pretty sure that Anniston Bennet was the key. I had to come to a deal with him, an understanding. But up until then I felt that he was in control of every interaction even though he was the one locked up.

I read Narciss's letter a dozen times while thinking in the back of my mind about Bennet.

She answered on the first ring. "Hello." It was 5:00 in the morning by then.

"Hey, Narciss," I said. "I just found your note."

"You're up early," she said.

"Let's have lunch tomorrow. You know, not later today but the next day."

"I don't know."

"The Japanese place in Sag Harbor is open for lunch, I think. Let's go there," I said.

"What time?"

"One-thirty. We can go at one-thirty and avoid a lunch crowd."

"I don't know if I should, Mr. Blakey."

"The name is Charles and don't think about it, just meet me. I won't bite and I won't make you see me again if you don't want."

"Are we going to talk business?"

"No. No business. I just want to clear up a couple of things."

She hesitated. I heard a tapping on her end of the line.

"I don't do much dating..."

"I just want to get together. It's not a date. It's lunch."

"Okay. One-thirty tomorrow."

"See ya then."

"Okay. Bye."

"Good morning, Mr. Bennet," I said at 6:45.

I snapped on the light and he jerked up from his mattress on the floor.

"Good morning."

I shoved the cold cereal and fruit under the door and sat on the trunk.

"Here's the deal," I said.

Bennet sat in his red chair and ran his hand down across his face until he was clasping his throat.

"Go on," he said.

"Everything is a privilege. Food is a privilege and so is water and light and the books to read. If you want me to be the warden of your life, then that's just what I'll be."

"How do I earn these privileges?" Bennet asked. He was very serious.

"I will ask you questions. And you will answer them. If

you refuse or I don't like your answers, then a privilege will be taken away. If I don't like your attitude, I will suspend privileges. If you lie, the same thing."

"But how will you know if I'm lying?"

"You will have to prove it to me."

For some reason that answer made Bennet flinch.

"And what are my rights?" he asked.

"You have only one right in here," I said. "At any time you can ask to be released. And then, ninety-six hours after that request, I will open the door and you can go."

"Don't forget your money."

"I don't care about the money. All I care about is my rules in my jail."

"And why the ninety-six-hour delay?"

"Because you're not going to be the boss here. This is my house. If you want to play some stupid game, you have to play by my rules. And believe me, if you say tomorrow that you want out, I will turn out the light and leave you down here with nothing but a mug of water for four days."

I believe that that was the first time I saw the true Anniston Bennet. All artifice was gone from his face. His brow knitted and his fingers did a jittery little dance.

"And if I don't answer your questions to your satisfaction?" he asked.

"Same thing," I said. "Solitary confinement. No light. Bread and water. For four days."

"What is this, Charles? Do you think you can break me?"

"This is my home," I said. "My home, my rules."

"How long do I have to think about this?"

"Right now. Right now. Either you say that you agree or I pull your ass outta there and drive you to the train station in those pajamas."

Underneath the glowering eyes a smile came to Anniston Bennet's lips.

"I will agree on one condition," he said.

"What's that?"

"Even though I might not exercise the option, I reserve the right to ask you one question for every three you ask of me. And you give me your word that you will answer as honestly as you can."

"Deal," I said.

"And if I answer the question you ask of me, that is, if you believe my answer, then I won't be punished because your question was inadequate. Also you have to ask specific questions and not something like *Tell me everything about this or that*."

"Okay," I said. I had already thought about the types of questions that would be fair. I agreed with his reservations.

I believed that if I couldn't ask the question, then I didn't deserve an answer. "Okay. I'll be specific and I will say why I don't believe something."

Anniston Bennet nodded his agreement. He was deadly serious. I can't even begin to explain how I felt.

PART THREE

PART TWELVE

twenty-two

"Why are you here?" I had brought him panfried scrod and boiled potatoes for dinner — that and a small pitcher of chilled Irish Breakfast tea.

"I don't understand."

It was the first jab and counter in our contest.

"Why do you want to be here in this cell in my basement? Why do you feel you should be in jail?"

Bennet had been sitting in his red plastic chair. He stood, held his hands out, and splayed his fingers. One hand was held high; the other was at waist level. They were like an ancient image of twin suns.

"Because, Charles. I am criminal." The suns turned to fists. "I have broken every commandment and dozens of laws and ordinances."

"What laws have —"

"It's my turn," he said.

"I only asked you one question."

"Why am I here?" he said, holding up a solitary thumb. "Why do I want to be here?" The forefinger. "And why do I feel I should be in jail?"

His count was correct, and I wanted to play by the rules.

"Did you embezzle money from Harbor Savings?" he asked.

My first impulse was to say no. I almost did. Then I wanted to say yes, but I couldn't get the word out of my mouth. I sat there, gritting my teeth. Bennet's only emotion was bland patience.

It dawned on me that I had gotten into a game that could lose. If I played by the rules we'd set out that morning, I was open to questions that made me just as vulnerable as Bennet. If I answered truthfully, he would have something on me.

And I couldn't be sure if what he told me was the truth.

"Yes," I said anyway. "Yes, I took money from the drawer. I guess you could call it embezzlement."

Anniston Bennet smiled.

"Have you ever murdered anybody?" I asked, expecting to wipe the smirk off his face.

"No," he replied, still showing his small teeth.

I stood up, knocking the standing book trunk flat on the floor behind me. "That's it!" I shouted. "Four days' solitary!"

He leaped to his feet also.

"That's not fair!" he cried, a bit playfully.

"Yes it is. You lied. I already know that you murdered that soldier in North Vietnam. Either you lied then or you are now."

"I did not lie on either count," Bennet complained. "I never said that I murdered that soldier. I said that I killed him, shot him actually. But I was ordered to do so by a legal representative of the government. I no more murdered that soldier than an executioner murders a condemned man."

"You said that you broke every commandment," I argued. But I realized before I finished that the commandment says *Thou shalt not kill*; it does not say *murder*.

"Are you a lawyer, Mr. Bennet?" I asked.

"No. I have no formal training as a lawyer and neither have I taken or passed the bar in any state or nation."

"What did you steal?"

"Only one thing," he said. "It was years ago, in the seventies in a villa outside of Rio de Janeiro. A painting that was just there leaning up against the wall in a poorly lit hallway that no one went into much. It was in a rich man's house. I was newly out of Asia and looking for a shipping connection outside the U.S. that would be willing to move what some saw as contraband. The man who owned the house also owned a dozen ships. Not big ships but big enough for my purposes. But it wasn't working out. The man either wanted too much or was scared and asked for too much, so I would have to abandon my efforts. I stayed a day or two too long. His daughter hated him. She would come up to my room every night and make love to me and tell me how much she hated him. She was the one who showed me the painting.

"It was a nude, a foot high and nine inches wide. She was peach colored and leaning over a blue chair. Picasso. Just threw it in my suitcase while Embado's daughter was sleeping in my bed. She slept late that day, and I managed to leave without waking her."

I allowed the idea to seep in. It wasn't the painting or Brazil or a beautiful young woman coming to him for sex in her own father's home. It wasn't any one of those things but all of them together. Thinking about his access to power and wealth, about his almost innocent lack of morals, set off an empty feeling in my chest.

I looked into his blue eyes while I thought of how to phrase my next question.

He saw what was going on in my eyes and said, "My turn."

I counted to myself and then nodded.

"Have you ever killed anybody?"

I wanted to get up and leave right then, to run away from Bennet — and everything else. I thought that I could free him and then I'd drive to New York. From there I could make it down to Atlanta, change my name, get a job unloading boxes.

But there was something about the peach-colored nude and the naked woman in the bed — something about me spending an entire lifetime up in my room reading comic books and masturbating while there was a real world outside that I was too scared to acknowledge. These things held me. Bennet's question was the deepest contact that I had ever had with another human being.

Brent was dying. He was almost dead already. The hospice nurse came in every morning to see about him. She changed his diapers and washed him. She fed him breakfast and then a volunteer would come later in the day to feed him dinner. The meals were the same, just a can of vitamin-enriched milk-shake-like stuff. Chocolate for dinner and banana in the morning. The nurse said that I should look in on him at night, but I never did — letting him sleep, I said to myself.

By then he couldn't even talk. He'd open his eyes when I'd come into the room though. He looked at me with longing eyes. Sometimes he'd hold out a feeble hand.

Before he was that far gone, Brent asked me to sit down next to his bed one morning. I had just brought in his breakfast and was getting ready to leave.

"Charles."

His voice was weak. I pretended not to hear him.

"Charles, please sit down for a minute."

I did as he asked. He took my hand.

"What?"

"I just wanted to say that I was sorry, boy. I just wanted to say that I know I treated you bad all these years. Called you names. Told you you were no good. I can see now that all that time what you needed was a father. That's why you were so bad. You were just mad and I never saw why. Can you forgive me?"

Tears came into my eyes. Tears of rage. The idea that Brent would mention my father, that he would dare to even suggest that he could have taken my father's place, made me hate him more than I ever had. I let go of his hand so as not to crack his fingers. He saw the tears and smiled. I believe that he thought I was forgiving him, that those tears were his absolution.

I wanted to deny it. I wanted to holler him into dust. I was so angry that I didn't trust my actions, so I left the room. I never spoke to Brent again. I didn't touch him again. I couldn't. The nurse was always telling me that a kind word or a gentle touch would be the best medicine.

But I couldn't touch him. I couldn't think of one kind thing to say. His smell made my stomach turn. I would have liked to jab knives into his eyes.

I didn't touch or talk to him; I didn't go into his room at night. Every day he got weaker and I thought to myself, *Good, I hope he dies soon. I hope he dies tonight while I'm in my bed thinking about the* Playboy *magazines that I stole from under his bed.*

One morning the nurse found him on the floor next to the door. He must have been trying to get out. Maybe he was trying to get to me. I heard something in the night, but I really thought that it was squirrels in the gutters, not my uncle scrabbling on the oak floor trying to escape from death.

The police asked me if I had heard anything. Everyone knew how much I hated Brent. But nothing came of it. He died of cancer. They couldn't arrest me for not being friendly, for rubbing my urgent erection on the mattress while thinking about impossibly endowed Tammy Lee Naidor, the Playmate of the month.

"No," I said to Bennet. "No, I've never killed anyone. And now I have to go. I'll come down tomorrow and ask you some more."

"Whatever you say, Warden." Bennet smiled.

"You want a book?"

"If I may," he said.

I passed him a paperback that I brought in my pocket. *Hothouse* by Brian Aldiss. It was a book set millions of years in the future, where plants had ascended to be the dominant species on Earth. Maybe I gave it to him because it was one of my favorites. I don't know.

I sat up at the head of my bed and communed with my ancestors. I didn't know a damn thing about them except that my family had kept and then forgotten them in the basement for hundreds of years. They were the only thing in my life of value right then — a hope that I came from somewhere important.

I was looking at the ivory faces and thinking about myself as an embezzler and a murderer. Brent had always called me a malingerer. Maybe I was that too.

Early in the morning, about 3:00 or so, I pulled out an old

spring binder that I had used in college. I started writing ideas for questions. By the time the sun came up, my tin trash can was filled with the failures I had penned.

twenty-three

Breakfast for the prisoner was shredded wheat and skim milk with no sugar and no fruit. I went in having resolved to deliver the food and leave.

I put the tray down and he said, "So what are we going to talk about today, Warden?"

"Is Anniston Bennet your real name?" I asked without thinking. But as soon as I asked, I was happy. It was only one question. I had to ask three before having to answer one of his.

I was so intent on the silly rules of the game that I almost missed Bennet's reaction. His head twisted to the right an inch or so and the skin around his eyes momentarily tightened into a network of fine wrinkles.

"Yes," he said.

But I knew better. The problem was that I had to ask another question to dig the truth out.

"Was it your birth name?"

"No."

"What was that name?"

"Tamal Knosos." He stared blue comets at me. No further information was forthcoming.

"It's your turn," I said.

"I'm thinking," he responded lamely.

"If you don't have anything to ask, then you forfeit and it's my turn again."

"Are you a child?" He sneered and frowned. I might have felt victorious at causing him to lash out like that, but there was a force behind his condemnation that unsettled me.

"No," I said. "And that was a question. So now you tell me where that name came from, why it was changed, and by whom."

I counted the inquiries on the same three fingers he had used the day before.

Tamal Knosos considered me for a long time. It took all of my concentration not to break away from his gaze. I knew somehow that if he stared me down, I would never regain the advantage.

Looking back on that morning, I can see how it might seem foolish, childish really, the game we played. Two full-grown men in that ridiculous situation. But if you were there, you'd have felt how deadly serious we were.

"I don't know," he said at last.

"You don't know what?"

"I don't know the answers, not the real answers. My mother's name was Maria Knosos, and she was unmarried. My father's name was Tamal. The birth certificate only had his first name. His nationality was Turkish. My name became Tamal Knosos because my mother died before she could give me a name. She had come to New York from Greece and met this man, Tamal, somewhere. He was already gone by the time I was born. I was neither Greek nor Turkish but an orphan in America. When I grew up I named myself. I didn't know a thing about either parent or their cultures. I was here and I meant to thrive. I created a whole history based on the name Bennet. The ancestors I chose came over on a boat before the American Revolution. They had died out mostly, except for Anniston, except for me."

I was looking closely at my prisoner. At his bald head and impossible eyes.

"Contact lenses," he said and then leaned forward, putting his fingers against his left eye. When he leaned back he had in his hand a big lens, whites and all, of a blue eye. The black eye that looked back at me from the left socket could well have been Greek or Turkish.

"I had my scalp done by an electrologist," he said. "In the kind of work I do, there's no promise that you will have a razor ready to shave the black locks."

"You're passing as a blue blood," I said. "But you're really nothing. You don't even know if your father was Turkish. He could have been Arab or even African."

"My name is Anniston Bennet," my prisoner said with conviction.

"It's your turn," I replied.

"I don't want to play this game anymore," he said.

"If you don't play my game, I don't play yours," I said simply. The power I felt was stronger than any alcohol.

Bennet replaced his blue eye and shook his head.

"You don't want to fuck with me, Charlie." He was another man again.

"Oh no?" I walked out of the basement and up to the house. In the pantry I had two loaves of white bread and three cans of Borden's condensed milk waiting for just this moment. These I carried back down into the hole. I shoved the food under the gate, smashing the bread in the process, and then threw a can opener through a cell diamond.

I went back to the hatch and snapped off the light. I called down, "See you in four days, Tamal."

He yelled something unintelligible as I slammed down the door to the cellar. He was still shouting as I secured the locks to the basement. But you could barely hear his shouts just five feet away from the hatch. It was a well-built stone cellar and the door was insulated, almost soundproof as it turned out.

I went up to the house listening for his shouts but heard nothing. At about noon I figured that he stopped, so I went back down to the cellar door. He was still shouting, loud and deep for such a small man.

I almost broke then. I almost threw the door open and set him free. I could have saved face by saying that I just wanted to throw a scare into him. I could have freed him and sent him packing. I knew that that was the wisest course to follow, but something else had taken me over. Perverse pride left Tamal/Anniston in his hole.

Ever since the first day he stood at my front door, I felt that Bennet held the upper hand. He was self-assured and a man of the world and rich and white. I was permanently unemployed and broke. Putting him in that cell and serving him was like tying Joe Frazier's right hand behind his back and then picking a fight with him.

The only way I could beat Bennet was to break him, to show him that I was boss of my house. To show him that I meant what I said and that I would not break down. After all, he agreed to my rules. He had said okay. What did he expect? He told me that he wanted to be punished, that he wanted me as his warden. I had warned him.

I was late getting out of the house and late to Tiger Tanaka's, the Japanese restaurant. Narciss was waiting patiently in the display window at a table for two.

"Hey," I said as I walked up. "Sorry I'm late. I had some business with Mr. Dent that I couldn't break off."

"That's okay." She smiled, looking down at first, and then in an act of will, she looked up for me to see her pleasure. "I was just thinking about the notes in your aunts' diaries. You know, I don't think that you should sell them either. So much of them is about everyday life in the black community out here, and there are names, names of your relatives back more than two hundred years."

"They got the guys that brought over those masks in there?"

Narciss beamed. "Not their names but there is a reference to three Africans that came over on a Spanish ship before the Revolution. I don't think these ladies knew about the masks. Now, either they didn't know of their relation to the three African sailors or somehow your family inherited the masks from another clan."

She was wearing a dark-blue dress that came to midthigh when she sat. It was a sharp number — new, I believed. I sat down, put my hands across the table, and touched her elbows with my fingers.

"I was thinking," she continued. "I mean, I haven't really pushed ahead with the sales yet. I was thinking that maybe you would like to start a museum."

"Museum?"

"Yes. An African American museum of the life out here. We could use my upstairs. I could charge admission. You wouldn't make as much as you would if you sold the pieces, but you could keep them and share them too."

"It's nice to see you, Miss Gully."

She struggled not to look away.

"What did you want to talk about?" she asked.

Her skin enchanted me again. The subtle variations of color gave depth to her.

"Oh, I don't know." Again words came out of my mouth as if they were uttered by some stranger. "I felt bad about how we got off the phone the other night. I like you and I was hoping that we didn't have to stop talking before we had a chance to be friends."

Narciss smiled and sighed. She touched her long fingers against my forearm, and the waitress, a blond teenager, came up to take our order.

I ate raw fish for the first time in my life. Yellowtail and tuna, and smoky and sweet-tasting sea urchin on a mint leaf. I paid for the meal and then took Narciss on a long drive out to Montauk. I kissed her the first time on the beach. We had been walking for more than an hour. She had done almost all the talking — mostly about the museum she wanted me to contribute toward — but there were details about her mother and father and her activist /lawyer sister, Rochelle, who lived in D.C. and had three children by as many men.

"She'd be a welfare mother if she wasn't a lawyer," she said at one point.

I was thinking that Rochelle didn't sound any different from many men that I had known. Men who bounced from woman to woman, creating babies as they went. Clarance was like that. There were at least three women who he admitted having children by. He was proud of his virility.

I was thinking about Rochelle's masculine approach, but I didn't care. Instead I stopped there on the sandy beach and kissed Rochelle's girly sister.

Narciss didn't resist. She had been waiting for it. Her left arm snaked up around my neck while her right hand gripped my biceps. Her tongue was quick to find mine.

We stood there in each other's arms until my legs began to ache. That was about 5:30. I broke away long enough to suggest that we drive back to my house. We made it to the car, but it was almost 7:00 before I turned the ignition key and started back toward home.

All that time we had only been kissing. Lips and necks. Her dress was sleeveless, so sometimes I kissed her arms. She leaned over me now and again, resting her forearm on my erection, but that was as close as we came to sex until we got back to my place.

The drive back was more than an hour. She filled up the minutes talking about my aunts' diaries and what importance they held.

"It's what real history is made of," Narciss said. She was reclining comfortably in her seat. The window was open and the wind blew across her face. "Recipes and funerals, petty disputes and detailed explanations of social gaffes. There's some talk about race but not as much as you'd expect. Your aunt Theodora was very religious, but Penelope and Jane-Anne hardly ever mentioned the Bible or the Lord. Just the leaves of the diaries under a glass case could be the room of a museum."

"I'll think about it," I said, reaching over to rest my hand on the upper thigh of her left leg.

She shuddered, but I didn't know if it was from the anticipation of sex or the chance she had to become a curator.

twenty-four

"Put your arms up over your head," I said to Narciss Gully.

We were both naked and lying on my mother's bed. She hesitated but then complied. I bound her wrists together with my left hand and proceeded to take her nipple in my mouth.

Her breasts were small, but the nipples were quite large. Though darker, they had the same multicoloring as the rest of her skin. The nipples were very hard against my tongue. I worked my hand down between her legs and flicked my finger against the moist flesh under the mound of hair.

"Oh God!" she hissed. "Oh no."

I continued to tease and nibble until her hissing turned into a shout.

"Oh God, oh no. Stop! Please. Too much."

"You want me to stop?" I asked while still licking her nipple.

"Please."

"First I'll count to five," I said.

"Oh."

"One..."

Narciss raised her head between her extended arms to look down at what my hand was doing.

"...two..."

She grinned and then grimaced ...

"...three..."

...and then slammed her head back on the mattress.

"...four..."

"I love you," she whispered.

"What?"

"Please. I can't take it."

"Five."

I released her and moved my teasing hand away. I stood above her and she turned over on her stomach, inviting me to lie down on her back.

"Do you hear something, Charles?"

I had just awakened in the dark room. Narciss was standing at the window, cupping her ear toward the pane.

I got up and went to her. It pleased me that she was still naked. I put my arm around her slender waist and she draped her arm on my shoulder.

"Listen," she said.

In the silence of night, you could barely make it out. No more than a murmur, it was only audible due to the proximity of my mother's window.

"It's that man again," I said.

"What man?"

"The man who lives out in these woods some summers. It's a hobo or something. Now and then someone calls the police, but they never find him. He's crazy, and sometimes when he drinks too much wine, he gets pretty loud. He keeps his distance though. You have to listen closely just to hear it at all."

"Have you seen him?"

"No, never."

"Then how do you know all of that?"

"I've found his camps and empty bottles of cheap wine. Some people have seen him too, but not me." My lies were becoming too large. I knew I should let it go, but I couldn't. "We called him the Padre when I was younger, because some folks said that he was preaching to the trees. He seems harmless enough."

I kissed Narciss and she forgot about Anniston Bennet's shouts and my lies.

Narciss needed to talk. She was very nervous about surrendering so completely to a man she hardly knew and told me so.

"The last time I fell for a man so fast, it was all wrong," she said as I was rubbing body oil into her shoulders. "It felt wonderful, but he wasn't the man for me."

"But he was right for a moment," I argued.

"He was awful. He would take things from my house."

"Really?"

"Yeah. A pearl ring, twenty dollars that I kept in a cookie jar, even large things like a toaster that I kept under the sink. At first I thought I was going crazy. But then one day I set a paper clip on the back of my jewelry box. He must have lifted the lid without noticing the pin. I knew immediately that he'd taken my zircon earrings. He did it three more times after that, and I broke up with him."

She pulled away from my massage and lay on her back. I reclined, resting my head on her small stomach.

"Why did you wait?" I asked. "Why didn't you get rid of him after the first time?"

She sat up, pushing my head down into her lap. I kissed her stomach. I remember because she had a ticklish reaction and then grabbed my hair to make me stop.

"It was weird," she said. "Like *The Twilight Zone*. I knew he was doing it, but he didn't know that I knew. I'd leave money in my purse or an earring on the night table and then he'd come in and do that love thing he did."

"It was that good?" I asked.

"He was a wonderful lover," she said. "But that wasn't why I kept him on for so long. It was like he was my shy prostitute, you know? He didn't want to feel like a whore, so I would let him steal from me and pretend that I didn't miss it."

I kissed her stomach again. This time she didn't grab my hair.

"So then why did you finally decide to break it off?"

"Because I started to change," she said.

"Change how?"

"I don't know if I should talk about it. I mean I don't even know you." Narciss stroked my head then, but I refrained from any more kisses.

"That's okay," I said. "I understand. We all have our secrets."

Really I didn't care about Narciss's secret sex life with her gigolo. I was thinking about the man in my basement, about what the consequences might be after he got out of his cell.

"It's not any kind of big secret or anything," she said. "It was just that I was acting like some other person and I didn't like who that person was."

"And who was that?" I asked, sitting up.

"I was aggressive. I made him do things and I asked him questions while we were . . . were doing it. I started calling him names and doing things that I never did before."

"What kind of things?"

She had finally caught my interest.

"I have to go to the bathroom." She stood up and walked out of my mother's door.

I went to the window and cupped my ear to the pane. It could have been a moose, maybe five miles distant. That's what I could have said.

I was tired and almost scared of what I had done to Anniston Bennet. I wondered if he had a strong heart — if the stressful time in my basement might kill him. I wanted to run down while Narciss was in the toilet and make sure that the prisoner wasn't dying. But then I thought that Bennet's death would make everything easier. No one knew where he was, he said. I could just put him in the ground in my family's plot. If no one was looking for him, he'd never be found. For a brief moment I considered leaving him down there until he died of starvation. If he died he couldn't get back at me.

When I realized that I was contemplating murder, I backed away from the window.

"Did you see him?" Narciss said from behind.

"No. No."

"Then why'd you jump away from the window like that?"

"I just remembered something. I have to go into the city tomorrow for a meeting. I thought it was the day after, but I just realized that I got confused."

"Oh." There was disappointment in Narciss's voice. "How will I get back to my car?"

"Don't worry about that," I said. "I'll give you a ride to your car when we get up."

"Oh." She hesitated. "I thought you were trying to get rid of me now."

"Why would you think that? You think I'd kick you out of my house in the middle of the night?"

"You've been so restless," she said. "I thought you wanted to be alone."

It was then that I realized what had happened to me. Really, what had happened to the world around me. Before Anniston Bennet had come into my life, I was invisible, moving silently among the people of the Harbor. No one wondered about me; no one questioned me. Even my best friends simply accepted what they saw. The card-player with a sharp tongue who couldn't back up half the things he said. The petty thief, the man across the street, dead Samuel's son. I might as well have been a tree at the end of the block. People saw me well enough to walk around, but that was just about it.

And for my part I treated everything and everyone around me in the same way. I could put a name on them, maybe. But I rarely touched or spoke a meaningful word to a soul. Weeks could go by and not one worthwhile piece of information would pass between me and another human being. The only chance I had at intimacy was with Clarance and Cat, but 90 percent of my time with them was spent under the influence of alcohol.

But now everything was different — half different, really. Still nobody saw me. The people at Curry's bar in East Hampton, people on the street in the Harbor. Bethany and Narciss saw something that was like me — an image of what I thought I wanted to be — but they had no idea what was on my mind.

What had changed was what I saw. It was as if everybody had become like a mirror, and I saw reflections of what they saw instead of what it was they were trying to show me or tell me. Narciss had become a mirror and an echo chamber, giving me back every word uttered and gesture made. And when I saw or heard something I didn't like, I had the chance to alter my behavior.

"No, baby," I said. "Not at all. I want to see you. I want you here. It's just that there's been so much on my mind, and I feel so comfortable with you that I kind of sink into it, if you know what I mean."

"What's wrong?" she asked.

But her nipples were tightening again, and I was feeling the beginnings of another erection.

"Let's go to bed," I said. I could have been an actor in an old black-and-white movie. An airplane ace or international journalist, world-weary and in need of quiet love.

She was in the movie too, and happy with her role. Arm in arm we walked back to the bed, moving together like choreographed dancers. Every kiss hit its mark and every breath was on cue.

twenty-five

Anniston Bennet stopped shouting sometime the next morning. After driving Narciss to her car, I went down to the hatch and listened, but there wasn't a murmur or sound. At first I thought about going in and checking on him, but then I decided that I should stick to my guns and make him wait the full ninety-six hours. I figured that he was still going to be mad no matter what, so I might as well do something worth him being mad.

I spent almost all of the next three days away from the house. The first night I hung out at Curry's bar, lying about my business and drinking up a storm. In the morning I got up early and started worrying about the sergeant that Bennet had slaughtered in North Vietnam.

But we aren't in Vietnam, I said to myself.

But he is a killer, I answered.

That morning I had made a date to go horseback riding for the first time in my life. I'd met a young white couple named Jodie and Byron. They were wealthy and invited me to come riding with them. I said that I'd never ridden before, but they promised that they'd show me how.

They had a girl they wanted me to meet. Extine was her name. She took me, along with Jodie and Byron, on a trip in woods around Southampton that I had never seen. Every inch of those woods is etched in my memory by the pain that saddle inflicted.

Jodie and Extine were cousins. Byron was Jodie's husband. They lived in the Hamptons every summer and fall and then spent the rest of the year between Aspen and Maui. Their money came from their parents. Who knows where it was before that?

Extine had big blond hair and big teeth that she presented in a permanent smile.

Extine loved horses. She told me that she had ridden every day of her life since the age of twelve.

"I love horses' hair and teeth and eyes," she told me two minutes after we met. "When I was a girl I'd sneak out of the house at night to sleep in the stables with my mare."

"It's great that you had something like that," I said. "I know a lot of people who never had something that they loved so much."

I was thinking about myself — about how I had wandered in and out of the same front door for thirty-three years without ever knowing which way I should have been going.

"Boy just like a housefly," Uncle Brent used to say. "So busy buzzin' he don't see the wall till it smack him upside the head."

"You don't think I'm crazy?" Extine asked with a sort of wonderment in her voice.

"I guess you could say that you were crazy," I said. "I mean *crazy* basically means that you're different from every-body else, and since you know what you want and most other people don't have any idea, then they got to call you crazy. But only because they're jealous."

Extine loved me after that. She was a big physical girl, just like her mare. All she wanted was to gallop and romp up and down the hot trails around the Hamptons.

She liked my company because I didn't think there was anything wrong with her obsession with horses. As a matter of fact I liked her because everything about her came down to horses. And a horse was an animal, like a deer.

Byron and Jodie took Extine and me to a *cabin* in woods connected to a property that was either theirs or a friend's.

It was a large place, and soon after dinner the big blond horsewoman and I wandered off to a secluded part of the residence.

That night we kissed a lot, but she didn't want to have sex. Extine was engaged to a guy named Sanderson who wouldn't mind if she kissed somebody, but he'd draw the line at intercourse.

I didn't care. My inner thighs were in deep pain. I was sure that I was bleeding on the inside. I fell asleep midkiss and didn't wake up until noon the next day. My new friends were all gone, leaving me miles away from anywhere without a car. I spent most of the afternoon walking down paths in an abandoned apple orchard, trying to find a way down to the road.

It was a hot day and I had to remove my sweater and top shirt. I was still in pain and limping, very thirsty too, I remember, and slightly panicked that I might die out there in the woods. The dirt of the path was bone-dry. The blossoms of the apples had begun their transformation to fruit. For a long time I hadn't thought about my prisoner, but on that desolate walk he came back to me.

A white man, maybe, who didn't know one thing about his past. Pure evil in the way of business. A thief and a killer by his own admission. Why did he want to be caged, anyway? He never really answered my question.

I thought that maybe I should disappear to Aspen or Hawaii. Maybe I should let the white man go and take his money and vanish.

I made it to a back road and finally got a ride to Curry's. There I sat and drank until closing time. When they kicked me out, I slept in my car and rose with the sun stabbing my eyes.

He could have been dead for all that I knew. But the deal was ninety-six hours, and I cracked the hatch on the second. The air in there was musty. I snapped on the light, and Anniston Bennet rose to his feet. He was bare chested but wore his bright-blue bottoms. Thick black hairs sprouted from his jaw, and there were gray bags under his eyes.

"Morning, Mr. Bennet," I said. "You ready to get outta here?"

His eyes, I noticed, were black, not blue. The absence of his contact lenses seemed to be saying something that I wasn't sure I wanted to know.

"I screamed for a whole day after you dropped that door," he said. "I kept it up like a chant. Must be pretty soundproof. After that didn't work I sharpened that can opener you left on the floor outside the cage. Then I made a slingshot out of the elastic in my other pair of pants. I was going to wait until you walked in and then I was going to shoot you dead."

I felt a drop of sweat as it went down past my left ear.

"But then I had to wait too long for you to come back, and the blood lust drained away." He sat in his red chair. "It's dark in here, you know. Black, actually, and the air gets thick when you don't open the door."

He passed the fingertips of both hands lightly over his eyebrows, then looked up at me. "You made me think about the things I came here to pay for. You made me wonder about the life that I thought I could repent. Little Malo from northern Uganda. A small chest of diamonds in Rwanda. There were tens of thousands there. But Malika, I think her name was Malika, was just one.

"You know, I've walked past death so many times that you'd think I'd somehow end up dead like that, but I haven't. Maybe I went a little crazy. I know a man in Connecticut who is willing to kill anyone anywhere in Africa or South America. He says he won't kill in this country or Europe, but life down south is open season for him. I know a man in the kidney business and another one who deals only in hearts."

"Is he black?" I asked.

"Who?"

"The assassin."

"Yes. Yes, he is. But that doesn't matter. He could be a white man. The fact is that he has become an individual, a man who takes actions solely from his own decision. Just like me, he is what he makes of himself. Maybe one day he'll fall apart too, but that won't matter either. You can never take back your life."

I didn't believe Bennet. His sorrow and self-pity, I thought, were a trick somehow. The only thing I couldn't figure was what he had to gain by fooling me now.

"Are you ready to go?" I asked.

"No."

"What you mean, no? You want another four days in the hole?"

He clasped his hands in front of his face as if in prayer and said, "I haven't done anything else wrong."

"What do you want from me, Mr. Bennet?"

"One time I walked into a room in Amsterdam wearing a polo shirt and khaki pants and changed the future of a nation," was his reply. "I once gave a nine-month-old infant as a present to a man's dog. The man wanted to see if the myth of wolves raising men could be true. I walked through a city of the dead, in Rwanda, guarded by soldiers who were paid in dollars. Everywhere men and women had lain for so long that their bones had softened and they had become deflated bags of maggots. I retrieved enough money in diamonds to rebuild a nation, but instead I took those jewels and put them in a titanium box in the Alps.

"I'm still a bookkeeper behind enemy lines. Do you understand that, Mr. Dodd-Blakey?"

"No, I don't."

"What did you do while I was down here?"

"I learned to ride horses and I got drunk and I got laid."

"Did you hear me screaming?"

"Sometimes. Not much though. You sounded like a moose who got stuck in some briar about a mile or so from here."

"Did you worry that I might die?"

"Some."

"Did you worry that I might kill you for treating me like that?"

"No," I lied.

"Have you ever watched a child being murdered, Mr. Blakey?"

I shook my head and squinted.

"I once made ten million dollars because I was willing to deliver one million to a man hiding from the communists in

Nicaragua. That's the American way." He laughed.

"Why are you here, Mr. Knosos?"

"Last summer I had a deal fall through."

I had gotten up to the gate and now I was shaking, too afraid to go further.

"You know," I said, "I don't think I need to know this."

"Let me stay a little bit longer, Charles," Anniston Bennet said. "You can take away the books and just feed me bread and water if you want. You can keep the lights off all the time, but please don't ask me to leave here."

"Are you crazy?"

"No. No, I'm not crazy at all. As a matter of fact I'm very sane. That's because I stopped for a minute and looked around and saw what it was that I was doing. All of a sudden I realized what was happening, what I had done was so, so..."

"...evil," I said, thinking that I was finishing his thought. "You realized that you were evil?"

Bennet was rubbing his fingers along the rough surface of his chin, considering my words.

"No, and yes. What had happened was evil. The child torn apart and half devoured by a dog in the night. Procuring a heart or a kidney for a man who I might need as a business contact one day. The act is evil." Bennet's face contorted to grapple with the concept he was explaining. "Yes. And my actions were also evil, criminal. But it was not me; it was the world around me. Not me but the commerce and the language of our world." He scooted up to the edge of his plastic chair and held his hands out separately, pinching the fingers together. "Death and starvation are integral parts of our language system, our form of communication. *Do what I say or else. Do your job or you're fired.* These words carry consequence. To avoid pain we comply. Or we don't and then we die. Our logic is evil, so the smartest and the most successful are devils. Like me. I am a good citizen and the worst demon. I realized it when a deal fell through. I failed and I had a dream and in the dream, I had done the right thing — failing."

"And so you're punishing yourself because you did good?" I asked.

He laughed. "Yes," he said. "Yes. Yes yes yes yes yes yes. I did the right thing and the whole world, my whole world, fell apart. I realized that the fact of my failure was good in one way. But even though thousands may have been spared, that is not important. In order for man to survive as a species, there has to be people like me. People have to die for others to produce. The deaths are wrong, but the continuation of the world is more important."

"So then you have been doing the right things. So there's nothing wrong with you. And if that's true then why would you feel that you need to be punished?"

Bennet sat back in his chair with all the certainty and fear of a despot awaiting his long-overdue execution.

"I was arrested once in Uganda. There was no trial; I was just taken to prison. I was beaten and tortured" — he leaned forward to indicate the scars on his shoulder — "and then left to contemplate my sins in a small cell. Pain is a part of life and I've always accepted the fact of death. But the time I spent in that cell, though I hated it while I was there, was like a gap in the thoroughfare that had been my life. Like the road just stopped and then there was a forest. A black forest, thick and dark, with no promise at all.

"My life stopped in that cell. And my worst enemy was everything that I knew. The blood work I've done. It was the worst experience I ever had. As the days went by, I got sick on the magnitude of what I had done. When they released me, I had to be hospitalized. I gashed my own thigh with a bayonet so that no one would realize how precarious my mind had become.

"As bad as that time in prison was, I wanted to go back — to face the evil and accept the accusations in my own mind. That's why I came here. I had no idea that you'd do the dictator one better by turning out the lights.

"I came here hoping to make a statement to myself. To isolate and punish the part of me who sees the evil. The only real way to be punished is to recognize and pay for your deeds. But when I was in that darkness, hating you, I saw everything all over again. I remembered checking the situation in Rwanda every day for over a year. We knew it was going to blow up down there. And then I remembered walking along the streets of the dead. In the darkness here, I can almost feel them. My own body odors are reminiscent of the smell of death. I could understand how the sweat and gasses become stronger when you die and then they leak out of you. And it's so dark and your heart is still beating, but death might be like that.

"I could not have stopped the massacre of the people there. I could not have changed the history set in motion centuries ago. And if I tried I would have lost all my power. I would have become like an ant under the foot of another man like me."

"I still don't get it, Mr. Bennet. Why here? Why me?"

"At first it was just a joke. Not a joke on you, Charles. I like you. You have a lot of potential. I chose you so that Anniston Bennet, the whitest white man that I could think up, would be jailed by a black man who really was a blue blood in American history. But then, when I got to know more about you, it seemed that you were my opposite in many more ways. You have done very little with your life, haven't you? No profession, no job. You have never completed one project. You've never made a woman pregnant or voted, as far as I can tell. You quit school.

"Your whole life could be called a failure. Every second up until this moment has been wasted. But still you are truly innocent while I, who have changed the course of nations, am not worthy to call you friend."

There was a fanatic tone to Bennet's words. Because of this I didn't pay much attention, at that moment, to the insults he gave me. Later on, after he was gone, I thought about what he had said. There wasn't much that I could disagree with. He was evil and I was a failure; maybe that was the difference between the good and bad people of the world.

"Can I stay?" he asked again.

"What do you expect to get out of staying down here?"

"I just don't want to leave yet, Warden. I need a little more time to think about all this."

"It sounds like you got it all figured out already," I said. "To save the world or whatever, you've got to be a badass."

"The words I say to you are just words. But the child I sold into death, the corpses I robbed — these are the truths that I can no longer avoid. I have to make peace with them. I have to make peace with them or I'll go crazy."

You're not too far from that already, I thought to myself.

"Just another week," he said. "Just seven more days."

"Let me think about it."

"Thank you, Charles. Thank you," he said.

twenty-six

I brought him breakfast and didn't unlock the cage, so he could stay for at least the day. Maybe I'd free him that evening — that's what I thought.

He wanted to talk more, but I refused. Just the few hints at the violence and pain he had caused set off a shaking inside me. I wandered around the floor of my house; then I tried to read a book. My mouth was producing too much saliva, and I had to swallow and spit continually. I had gas pains relieved only by foul-smelling farts. My fingers and toes felt numb. My teeth hurt at the gums.

I was scared to death. I felt like a man riding an avalanche; it was only a matter of time before I'd be plowed under and crushed.

I wanted my mother or father. Even a bad word from Uncle Brent would have been a relief from my fears. I went to the liquor cabinet but couldn't stomach the idea of drinking.

Finally I sat down on the floor in the middle of the living room and closed my eyes. It was something I had done when I was a small boy. When everything got too exciting, I'd sit on the floor and think about the shadows on my eyelids. On a sunny day the darks and lights, the blues, grays, and reds that appeared behind closed eyes were like the ocean. I imagined myself as a little octopus, seeing the sea world and feeling safe because I had so many arms. Sometimes I'd make up little songs, humming a tune about nothing and floating in the ocean among fishes and sea kings.

I had crossed over from turmoil to childish ecstasy by the time the doorbell rang. I don't know how long I had been sitting, but my feet were asleep and it was painful and slow for me to rise. I didn't know how long the bell had been ringing either, but it stopped before I could hobble to the front door. I remember laughing at my exaggerated limp. *Like an old man*, I thought. And for some reason that made me happy.

She was headed back down the front stairs. Across the street, Miss Littleneck was watching.

"Extine," I called out.

The woman with the big blond hair hesitated a moment and then turned around.

"Hi," she said. "I came over to say that I was sorry."

She was wearing jeans and a button-up blue-cotton blouse that didn't cover her midriff. Both articles of clothing were tight. She had yellow rubber flip-flops on her feet and a yellow-and-white scarf around her neck.

Just thrown together, Uncle Brent's voice said in my memory.

"Come on in," I invited. She accepted with a bowed head.

"How did you find where I lived?" I asked Extine in the breakfast nook next to the kitchen. I had poured her some apple juice, which she wasn't drinking.

191

"Petey said that he knew a guy who knew where your house was," she answered.

Petey was the regular bartender at Curry's. Somebody in town must have recognized me.

I was struck and scared by her appearance at my door.

It's not that I cared about Extine finding me, but I realized that my feeling of invisibility was false. People did see me. They knew when I passed in the street. My actions were noted no matter how small I thought I was.

"So I decided," she continued, "to come over and apologize for leaving you out there like that."

"Why did you leave me?" I asked.

"Jodie and By left and I told them that I would drive you home. They were mad at me because they thought I slept with you, and Byron and Sanderson are friends. I don't know. I guess I got mad at you. I thought that you had taken advantage of me..."

"I passed out," I complained. "And then you left me without a ride."

"You put your hands on my breasts and jerked me by the arm," she countered. "I thought you were going to rape me."

"I don't remember," I said. And I didn't. "I remember kissing you. I remember that. But I thought that that was okay. I thought you liked it."

"That doesn't mean I wanted your hands all over me." She was getting angry. I could see that she was deeply bothered.

"I'm sorry, Extine," I said. "It was a bad mix — whiskey and horsehair. Please accept my apology. You know I didn't want to make you mad."

"Okay," she said as if it was the apology she had come for. "And I'm sorry too, about leaving you out there with no way to get home."

"Why did you leave me?" I asked again.

The question surprised her. By her face I could see that she thought the answer was obvious.

"I mean," I continued. "Did you think that you just wanted to get away from me? That you couldn't stand one more minute in my company and you just had to leave? Or was it that you were mad at me and wanted to hurt me by making me walk all those miles lost in the woods?"

She thought about the question for a moment, and then a moment more.

"I don't know," she said. "I was mad. I didn't want to see you. And I didn't know what you would be like in the morning all alone out there. When By and Jodie left, it was only you and me. I was afraid, I guess."

"Afraid that I'd hurt you?"

"I guess."

"Then why did you come here?"

"I felt guilty. That's why."

"Guilty because you kissed me? Or guilty that you left?"

Extine frowned and did not answer.

I stood up and she scrambled to her feet.

"Don't worry," I said. "I wouldn't have hurt you even in those woods. I'm a safe Negro. You could put a soap bubble in my hand and it'd never even pop."

Extine liked neither the sound of my voice nor the words that I said.

"I have to go," she said.

"Yeah. I know."

I watched her drive away in a convertible Jaguar sports car. I don't remember the model, but it was expensive, no doubt.

"Charles," Miss Littleneck called from across the street.

"Yes, ma'am?"

"Who was that white girl?"

"Just somebody I met."

For a long time after she was gone, I thought about Extine. Her presence, her kisses, meant very little to me. Our physical relationship, what little of it there was, was no more than an exercise. I realized that most physical intimacy was like that for me. I liked sex, but it was only a bodily pleasure. It wasn't an expression of love but just a need, a pleasant moment, sometimes even a chore.

What mattered about Extine was that she sought me out, that she found me. All of the women I had gotten to know after meeting Anniston Bennet had that in common. They made me real by seeking me. It's not that they knew what they were looking for. Bethany only liked me because I resisted her erotic power. Extine ... Extine liked horses, and at the end of a satisfying day in the saddle, she found me at her side. Narciss called me Mr. Blakey. She refused to see the solitary and jobless man who hadn't accomplished one thing in his entire life.

It wasn't that she was trying to form me with her blindness. She could only see in me what she needed. But because of the purity of her vision, I changed. I didn't become what she needed, but the force she exerted on me — the impact of her desire — caused love of a sort. Not the kind of feeling that would bring us together but love still and all.

To a lesser extent I was changed by Bethany and Extine. We had shared a moment of transformation — like in one of my science-fiction novels.

After going through that long tunnel of thought, I emerged realizing that I could now answer Anniston Bennet's question about love.

I went straight to the cellar and found Mr. Bennet with an erection. You could see the enormous arching contour under his hand-washed prison pants. I imagined that he had been masturbating when I opened the hatch and didn't have time to calm down. I didn't ask him about it though. I had more important things on my mind.

"Did you really sell a baby to a man's dog?" I asked even before perching on the trunk.

I had thought that we would talk about love. I hoped to impress him with my self-realization. But once I understood my own impulses, I found that I was hungry for more understanding.

"Yes," Bennet answered in an almost silent whisper.

"Did you know about Rwanda before it happened and didn't say a word?"

"Yes," he said a little louder. "But that's different. Everyone knew that it was about to explode down there. Saying words wouldn't have mattered. I don't know if anything I could have done would have made a difference."

"And you stole that painting?"

He nodded.

"...and killed that sergeant?"

He nodded again.

"...and you bought human organs from a man who dealt in that trade?"

Bennet hesitated a moment and then nodded again.

"But you still don't think you're a murderer? Even though somebody's got to die to give up a heart."

Bennet almost answered that but then swallowed and stayed silent.

"What was your failure?" I asked him.

"I thought you didn't want to know about that?"

"I don't," I said. "But I have to. I have to know what I got down here. I can't be too afraid to ask."

"Why not, Charles?"

"Because it's here. I took your money and now I have to know what I sold."

Bennet's face was filled with an emotion that I could not decipher.

"It was a device," he said. "A device that could cause terrible damage if put into the wrong hands. I knew about a youthful indiscretion of a man who had some overseas contacts, influence. We knew each other socially, as chance would have it. But it was through e-mail, anonymously, that I delivered my threat. It wasn't blackmail exactly because he stood to become a wealthy man with our transaction. But circumstances threw the deal out of whack. It didn't work out."

"What circumstances?"

"A case of conscience and subsequent suicide." Bennet's words were completely emotionless.

"So he saved his name without giving in to you." I felt the victim's triumph.

"He didn't give in," Bennet agreed. "But his secret was still leaked. It was in all the papers nine months ago. I had to punish him even though he was dead because there would be other candidates and they should realize that consequences go beyond the grave."

"You *are* evil," I said.

"I'm a tool, Charles. A precision tool. A tool of destruction. A tool of the dollar and the euro and the yen. But my actions are not mine alone. All the possibility of the world exists without me. That man would have died anyway. And the target of that device will one day be destroyed. That's the way of the world. It's not a question of good or evil. It's a question of humanity and what is done in that name."

"Then why put yourself down here?" I asked again.

Bennet's erection was gone. He winced and grimaced, clutched his hands into fists.

"Don't you understand yet? I can't explain it like the instructions to put together a box. It's powerful stuff. Powerful stuff. Powerful enough to destroy."

"Do you want to get out of here?"

"No."

"Will you answer my question?"

"I've already answered as well as I could."

"I don't believe that. So you either answer me right now or leave or spend four more days in the hole."

"I can't leave and I've already answered."

I brought him more bread and condensed milk, which I opened for him since I had confiscated his opener. Then I left him with ninety-six more hours to contemplate his crimes.

twenty-seven

Around that time I started putting money in banks in South-ampton, East Hampton, out down in Long Island City. Five hundred dollars at a time in interest-bearing savings accounts. I dated Bethany, Extine, and Narciss three of the four nights that I avoided the hatch behind my house. Extine spent the night wanting to kiss me, but I refrained because I knew that would take her power away. Narciss and I went to see the remastered version of Orson Welles's *Touch of Evil*. Afterward we talked about it and then I drove her home. She asked me to come in, but I said no.

"Don't you like me?" she asked with excruciating honesty.

"I do, honey. But I'm like an athlete in training. I need all my power to concentrate."

"Training for what?"

"An examination. A test that Mr. Dent is giving me."

"What kind of test?"

"Just to see what I know, what I can do."

"Like an aptitude test?"

"Uh-huh. Just like that."

Bethany was the biggest problem and the most fun. I took

her to the fanciest restaurant we knew, the Captain's Table in Amagansett. I told her up front that I was going home alone, and she proceeded to spend the rest of the night being all sexy and seductive. Every move of her shoulders set my heart to thrumming.

I kissed her for a long while at her door. But then I told her that I had to get home, that I had an important meeting the next day. And that was no lie.

Every night I sat up late with my ancestors. Leonard, the geeky-looking one, JoJo, the warrior, and Singer, the mask with his lips set into an O. I named them and thought about them. I had made up their characters and histories, but they were real to me.

Singer was a priest. He knew songs all the way back to the first songs. He was from the Congo, I believed, and not related to Leonard, who dealt in slaves, or JoJo, who protected Leonard even though he knew what his brother did was wrong.

I talked with them in earnest for hours. JoJo's voice told me that death was nothing to fear. Leonard suggested that I get the money while I still had the man locked away and powerless.

Singer I did not understand. His placid face always chanting. I learned the most from him.

I wasn't crazy. It's just that my world had disintegrated. Or maybe it was that I never really had a life but hadn't known it, so I was blissful in my ignorance. Everything began to fall apart when I started talking to Anniston Bennet... No. Before Bennet and I started our talks on evil, when I started cleaning out my cellar... Or maybe it went all the way back to Uncle Brent or before him to when my father died.

*

I put on a dark suit with a yellow shirt and a splashy red-and-blue tie to go see Bennet. His beard was filling in and his dark eyes were intense. It took him a full five minutes to get used to the light. He had lost weight, and from the smell of the room, I thought he might have had an intestinal disorder.

I didn't care about any of that. It wasn't my choice, I felt, but his. He could walk free at any time or answer my questions and eat steak.

"Mr. Bennet," I said.

"Mr. Dodd-Blakey."

"Are you ready to answer my questions?"

"Don't you mean am I ready to go home?"

"Not before you answer my questions."

I thought that there were tears in his eyes, but I wasn't certain.

"Why do you want to be down here in this cage?" I asked.

"Don't you see? Haven't you been listening to me?" he said. "With a word from me, your life could end. Maybe just with a gesture. A sentence could level a city block or blow a jetliner out of the sky. A dream could destroy Philadelphia. A disagreement could throw western Africa into famine for five years. You see it every day on TV, but no one listens. People like me move around, but no one knows our names."

"Maybe you're hiding down here," I suggested.

"I'm not afraid to die, Charles. I've truly walked through the valley of death."

"If you aren't hiding, then are you afraid of what you might do?"

"There's nothing I can do. Nothing."

"I don't understand. If you feel like you don't make a difference, then why torture yourself?"

Bennet looked at me with wide frightened eyes. "Don't

leave me in the dark again, Charles. Give me a couple of days with some food and light."

"All you have to do is answer my question, Mr. Bennet."

"Give me a couple of days."

"Could that baby ask you that?"

Maybe I was crazy. I didn't hate Bennet. I was his employee. Somehow I felt that he was still calling the shots, that he was making up his own mind to starve in darkness four days more. He was tortured behind those black eyes, under that scorched head. I was the tool of his penance.

He was a slaver of souls in the twentieth century. He was a killer and a liar and a thief, but that didn't matter to me. From what he had said I understood that he was a torturer of black people, but I believed him when he said that it wasn't out of malice or even intent.

My domination of him came from a personal conflict we were having. I didn't want to be another one of his slaves. I was foolish enough to believe that I could take his money and keep my freedom.

The next four days were spent pretty much as the last. I saw a lady three out of four nights. The first day I went fishing and didn't catch a thing. The next day I saw Clarance and Ricky together for the first time in months. I picked them up in my car and treated them to drinks at the American Hotel in Sag Harbor. We sat in the front room talking about old times and drinking port. Clarance smoked a cigar.

"What's goin' on with you?" Clarance asked me in the middle of our talk.

"What you mean?"

"I mean you never answer your phone and we don't see you. You don't have a job, but you're still in your house and goin' out buyin' port. Somebody said that they saw you at Curry's in East Hampton. One guy saw you hitch-hiking down the road to Southampton."

"I don't know, Clarance," I said. "Things are changing. You know I haven't done much with my life and I'd like to change that if I could."

"What you gonna do?"

I knew the answer to his question right then, when he asked, but I didn't answer because secrets had become dearer to me than their own content or designs.

The pecan pie was the most unexpected thing that happened while I waited for my prisoner to soften up in the dark. I bought the pie, which was edged in chocolate, at a roadside bakery stand that my mother used to frequent. It was a beautiful pie. The pecans crowded the surface and the crust rose like a collar, leaving ample room for the chocolate edge.

I bought the pie in memory of my mother, but when I got home I carried it across the street to Miss Littleneck. She was delighted and insisted that I come in to share the gift of giving with her sister, Chastity.

The entranceway to the Littleneck home was close and unlivable, I thought. Irene led me up a flight of narrow stairs to a room where the scent of death hovered like incense. In the small bed lay a woman, once black and now gray, the size of a child and wearing a curly brown wig. Her eyes might have been open. Her chest didn't seem to move. But I knew from the jittering finger of her left hand on top of the blanket that she was still among the living, at least for a little bit and a while.

"Chastity, look what little Charles Blakey brought us," Irene Littleneck said. "He brought us your favorite pie. And he didn't even know that you liked it. Did you, Charles?"

I shook my head.

"Speak up, Charles," Irene ordered. "Chassy doesn't hear so well."

"No," I said. "I didn't know you liked the pie, but I hope you like it."

"Isn't that nice?" Irene asked her sister.

The dying woman's fingers got a little more agitated. Irene held her sister's wrist and peered down into the half-closed eyes. "He's a godsend, don't you think?"

The one-sided talk went on for a while. Then Irene turned to me and said, "We better let her get some rest. You know, she hasn't had a guest in more than three years."

"Mr. Bennet."

"Mr. Dodd-Blakey."

Anniston Bennet was sick by this time. His eyes had trouble keeping their focus even after they had become accustomed to the light. Only half a loaf of bread had been eaten and he was unwashed. If I had not just seen Chastity Littleneck, I might have broken down right then.

"Why do you torture me?" he asked.

"Why don't you just leave?"

"I don't know. I can't tell. I'm supposed to be down here. Trapped by a Negro, a black man, until the bubble in my brain passes. Until the itch in my heart goes away."

He said all of that staring down at my feet. Again I didn't believe him. Anytime he showed weakness I thought it was a trap.

"That's no answer," I said. It was a phrase my father used when I avoided his questions.

"I swear it is," Bennet said. "There's a bubble in my brain, not a tumor but I can feel it. And I want to tear my chest open. Did you know how far a woman would go to save her babies from starvation?"

The last question took me by surprise.

"Say what?" I asked.

"That's what you want to know," Bennet said. "There was a rich man somewhere on the Mediterranean who wanted to experiment on a child. A thousand miles south of him, there was a political campaign of famine being waged. And among the population there were many mothers who would have jumped at the offer of feeding the rest of her family at the cost of one son. I was just a conduit, a wire making the circuit. If one child had not died, the whole family would have perished."

"You could have saved them all," I said.

"That time maybe. And maybe I did once in a while. But the power is drained away if you never meet your obligations. The rich man I aided gave me power that some presidents wouldn't have understood."

"Is it the guilt over that child that brings you here?"

"No. I don't think so. Can I have some oatmeal?"

I made his afternoon meal of porridge and returned to watch him eat.

"Can I have light tonight?" he asked me.

"You could go home and sit next to a fire."

"I don't want to go. I have to wait out the time."

"Then you can stay, but I want to hear everything. No more games."

twenty-eight

No matter what it might sound like, I hadn't become heart-less. For the next three days, I fed Bennet porridge, bananas, and other soft foods that would strengthen him.

I sat with him for hours just talking and keeping him company. We played chess (which he always won) and talked about stock investments that I should consider.

He got back some of his color and gained a pound or two.

One afternoon I went to an electronics store and bought a long-play tape recorder that was small enough to strap to my back. The tape had a two-hour capacity and I could pin the microphone to the sleeve of my shirt.

"Okay," I told my prisoner on the fourth day, the secret tape recorder running, "let's go over everything you've done."

"Why do you want this?" he asked.

"Because you forced your way down here and got all in my life. You know everything about my crimes and misde-meanors. You tell me that my cellar is your prison. Well, all right, fine, what are you in here for? What have you done?"

He smiled slightly. That's how it began.

I have his confessions on tape in a secret place in the basement. I keep it hidden behind a stone in the wall. The crimes he detailed to me were fantastic and sick. He robbed Peter to kill Paul. He was at the center of much suffering that I never even knew existed.

"You think that you can have the easy life of TV and gasoline without someone suffering and dying somewhere?" he asked me. Then he told me about the execution of three hundred loyal officers that one dictator realized might turn against him one day. He had nothing to do with the killings, but he was in that Central American country at the time, making liaisons with that government for a fruit concern in the Midwest. He knew the plan before it was executed but did nothing to stop it.

"It was not my business," he said.

"But could you have stopped it?" I asked.

"Not without killing every man, woman, and child in this world," he answered. "And it's not really worth it, you know. Saving lives."

"What do you mean by that?" I asked.

"I saved a man once," he said. "He was a journalist in the south of Africa. For the crime of writing against a mineral conglomerate, he was framed, arrested, and sentenced to death. I went to him on behalf of his sister. She worked in an office I kept in Rhodesia. She begged me to help. I liked her a lot so I told her that he was doing what he had to do, but she still begged me. I went to him and told him what would happen after he died. How the rest of his friends and his loved ones would suffer. When he refused me I told him that I would have to give his sister's name to the army because she was working against them too. All he had to do was agree to keep silent and the mineral company would forget him and give him money to migrate off the continent."

"Did he agree?" I asked.

"Yes."

"So you saved him."

"He died from drink in Morocco in just two years. You can't save fools and you can't save victims. That's why I've got this bubble in my head. It's like every step is planned from the beginning."

Weeks passed. Every day I spent down in the basement with my prisoner and my secret tape recorder. That's how I began to think of him. My prisoner. As long as he was in that basement, I figured that the world was a little safer place. I was also his confessor, the chronicler of his sins.

After hearing about hundreds of crimes, I decided to ask about Bennet's own past.

"Did you ever find out who your father was?" I asked.

"I'd rather not talk about that."

"Would you rather four days in the hole?"

Bennet was afraid of the dark by that time. He had experienced something down in the darkness that scared him. I knew he wouldn't refuse my questions. I had dominated him with the fear of isolation.

At that time I felt that my actions were justified.

"I don't know who my father was. Except that he really was from Turkey and that he was murdered after making my mother pregnant."

"How do you know that?"

"I hired a detective to search for him. He found that a Tamal Hikmet was murdered in Harlem buying heroin eight months before I was born. Tamal was a Turkish illegal. He was an addict and a playwright. No one could have saved him. No one can save anyone, not even themselves."

"But maybe they can be redeemed," I suggested. To my

knowledge that was the first time in my life that I had ever used a derivative of the word *redemption*.

"What does that mean?"

"Maybe they can make amends for their crimes. Maybe they can make a stand. Tell the world what is right."

"You ever read *Moby Dick*, Charles?"

I had not and shook my head to say so.

"There's a cook in that book," my prisoner said. "A cook who lectures to sharks about their nature. He tells them that they could be angels if they just mastered their appetites. He preached to them, but they didn't understand. Our hearts are like those sharks. There's no curbing the appetite of a hungry heart."

"Maybe he was talking to himself," I said, not thinking really, just making up words.

But Mr. Anniston Bennet, Tamal Knosos, aka Hikmet, looked up at me with something like wonder in his face.

He wrestled with the words that I had already forgotten and then repeated them and then wrestled some more.

"Talking to himself," he said a third time.

Anniston Bennet was a murderer if you went by his words. He had people killed, and he killed with his own hands four times. Never in self-defense — he was a predator with no natural enemies. But he never killed without the say-so of officials in the government; he never killed for passion — at least that's what he said.

When his time in my cellar was almost up, he became jaunty. He made jokes with me and said thank you every night before I left him.

I was happy then too. I had three girlfriends, money in the bank, and plans for my future, and I was friends with

Clarance and Ricky again. Some weeks earlier I told Narciss that I wanted my family heirlooms back so I could make a museum out of my ancestry in the house where that family throve.

Every now and then Bennet would say to me, "The cook was talking to himself, huh, Charles?"

"I don't know," I'd say to him. "I just said it. You're the one who read the book."

He'd smile at me and sit back in his red chair. He had a full beard by then, and he never wore his blue contacts at all.

It was his last Thursday in my home when I came down to see him. I opened the hatch and was greeted by silence. Usually I could hear the rustle of his movements, his standing or rising from his cot. But that Thursday he did not rise. He stayed sleeping in his bed.

"Mr. Bennet," I said, but he made no motion.

I said it louder with no more effect.

By the third time I was frightened.

By the fifth I went back to my house to find the key to his cage.

Anniston Bennet was dead. Peaceful and placid, lying with no blankets, dressed only in his self-styled prison pants. Under his bed was a neat stack of envelopes that were sealed, stamped, and addressed to different people, including me.

There was no wound or other sign of trauma. He had just gone to sleep and drifted off to death. I never even considered calling the hospital. His body was already stiff.

The letters were addressed mainly to people in New York City and Washington, D.C. But there were envelopes destined for Europe and Africa, Asia and South America too.

I opened only the one addressed to me.

Dear Charles:

Or should I say Warden? You have found me now, dead, in your basement. I wonder what you will do with my corpse? I have left letters for my business associates and the two friends I have. There are also notes for two wives and children. I have said goodbye to all of them. It would be nice for you to send them.

But I know you may not be inclined to let out the news of my death in your custody. There may be those who will feel uncertain about your part in my death. And though no one will hold you responsible, they might worry about what I told you, seeing how crazy this suicide might seem.

There is one pill left in the glass on the floor. It is a fast-acting poison called Sleeper that was designed to be painless. I leave one for you in case you one day feel at an end.

I had the pills, but I wasn't sure when I came to you that I wanted to die. I mean, I've wanted to die for a long time now, but I could see no reason until you left me in the dark. In the dark they all came back to me. The dead people and the fools. The women who gave themselves for money and the men who gave themselves for women. The old men who couldn't even get it up anymore who gave themselves for power. And me like a sheepdog keeping them in line, leading them to slaughter because it was what I was asked to do.

I smelled blood in the darkness. I heard the silence of death. And then a light would come and you would walk down the stairs asking if the ones I killed were black men just as if death had a race. I began to like you. Even though you turned on me and beat me with the darkness and silly questions.

When the confessions were all through, I knew there was no more to say. You left just a few minutes ago. I will take the Sleeper after this one last letter (the rest I've written over the past two weeks).

210

I want to die telling you something, Charles. I want to pass something on, but I can't think of a thing. Now that death is coming the bubble is gone, the itch in my heart has subsided and there's nothing left to think.

The only words I have to pass on are the ones to a story I never told you.

I once had to kill a man (a white man) — my boss. The man who brought me into reclamations after I was finished with government work. His name was Stewart Tellman and he was from Greenwich too. He taught me everything that I tried to tell you. I learned from him and we did good business. But one day his grandson was killed by a falling beam at a construction site. A hydraulic lift went out of control.

Stew had the man working the lift murdered. Then he started making crazy decisions on the job. He took chances and left clues of our coming. He spent hours sitting in the dark like you made me do for days.

I went to his home one night while his wife was away visiting their daughter. I came in a window and shot him in the head. He was napping. His head was down on a mahogany desk in the study. I shot him and it wasn't murder. He had killed himself as far as I was concerned.

I sat with him all night watching his blood congeal and his skin tighten. I knew then (seventeen years ago) that one day I would have to die like that. I decided to do it myself rather than leave it for someone else.

But I couldn't have done it without you, Charles. You gave me the time to say goodbye. The rest of your money is in a false bottom of my book trunk.

Tamal

The next few hours were the hardest I ever knew. The man in my basement was dead. A corpse that I could never explain. I sat with him all day and into the next night. When it was late I went out into the graveyard and dug a hole between my great-great-grandfather William P. Dodd and my aunt Theodora. I dug all night long, wondering if Miss Littleneck was hiding in the bushes, spying on my crime.

I covered the hole with two doors that I took off the hinges of the two toilets in my house. The next night I dug some more. The hole was as deep as I am tall before I dragged the board-stiff corpse from my basement. I rolled him in and covered him over. There was no ceremony.

The following day I dismantled the cell. Over the next few weeks I used a blowtorch and an electric saw to cut the metal into pieces, which I deposited, along with the dismantled toilet, in dump sites around the island. I burned his trunk and books and clothes.

All that was left of him were those letters and about forty tapes of his confessions.

He was right; I never sent his letters. I buried them with his tapes in the basement where he died.

I started my museum. Now, with Narciss, I collect pieces of black history from the area where I live. Narciss and I don't go out anymore. I told her that I'm not monogamous but I'd still like to be friends. After a while she came around.

I make my money from admission fees and from the historically black colleges that send up graduate students and professors now and then to study my collection. Narciss is good at applying for grants, so we usually have enough to pay our salaries.

Chastity Littleneck died and I was the only one other than Irene and the minister at the funeral. The whole time I kept thinking that it was Anniston Bennet's funeral I was attending. It was sad, but I didn't cry.

Irene died four weeks later. She left me her house in a new will. It was that one pecan pie and a walk in the graveyard. Bennet was wrong but he would never know it. Some people live according to love and being loved — if only a little.

I rent the Littleneck house to rich people in the summer. And I still live up in my childhood room, playing cards on Thursdays (closing the museum early) and doing very little to make life grand.

Extine went away at the end of the season. If she ever came back she didn't call me. Bethany married Ricky. Clarance was his best man.

I don't think I'll ever get married. I still haven't found love, and whenever I think about children, I remember that there once was a boy who was sold to a dog.

Also by Walter Mosley and published by Serpent's Tail

An Easy Rawlins Mystery
Devil in a Blue Dress

'A brilliant novel. Period' Jonathan Kellerman

'A first novel of astonishing virtuosity, upending Chandler's LA to show a dark side of a different kind' *Sunday Times*

'Mosley promises to manipulate the genre to accommodate a genuinely original vision – a hidden history of life in black LA from the Forties to the Eighties' *The Face*

'There is a splendid freshness to Mosley's prose and we sense that here is a real world we are hearing about for the first time' *Financial Times*

'For a writer who has the legacy of Chester Himes and more to live up to, Walter Mosley makes a distinctly confident start to his career' *Time Out*

'What really makes this novel is the writing... great stuff' *i-D*

The time is 1948. The town is Los Angeles. The hero is Easy Rawlins, an out of work black war veteran. The mortgage payment's coming due, so Easy accepts the assignment of finding Daphne Monet, blonde torch singer. In his search through a sleazy, fearful city, he is lucky to be under the protection of the murderous Mouse...

Published in 1991, *The Devil in a Blue Dress* was awarded the John Creasey Award for the best first crime novel of the year. It immediately established Walter Mosley as one of the great contemporary American writers.

What Next: A Memoir Toward World Peace

'African Americans, in particular, have used the excuse of America's racism and lack of political inclusiveness to absolve themselves of responsibility for her actions. But for Mosley, there is no such absolution, no safe haven where African Americans can shirk responsibility for the wrong done in their names. "It is up to me to make sure my dark-skinned brothers and sisters around the world have what I have," he asserts. "That they are not enslaved, vilified, or raped by my desire to eat cornflakes or take a drive to the shore" ... Mosley's words will resonate with any American who questions our government's geopolitical motives and methods in these unsettling times' *Los Angeles Times*

Starting with a memory of his father Leroy's experiences in World War II, Walter Mosley writes passionately about the need for Black people to become active in the struggle for world peace. He argues that because of their experience of oppression Black people are crucially placed to build bridges between the affluent first world and the impoverished third world.

Based on the personal insights that are the hallmark of his fiction, *What Next* is Walter Mosley's moving call to action. In the tradition of Noam Chomsky and Naomi Klein, *What Next* is a generous book that reminds us that we are all part of a wider community of interests that requires nurturing and support.

Always Outnumbered, Always Outgunned

'A startling exploration of the poverty and violence of black ghetto life...stunning' *The Good Book Guide*

'Unputdownable tension... This is traditional Americana, plain-spoken, written with a poet's precision, and astonishingly moving' *Independent*

'An extraordinary portrait of a sub-society made up of no money, petty crime, basic sex and ambivalent morality' *The Times*

Outstanding' *Daily Telegraph*

'Socrates thought about a promise he'd made. He swore to himself that he'd never hurt another person – except if he had to do it for self-preservation. He swore to try and do good if the chance came before him. That way he could ease the evil deeds that he had perpetrated in the long evil life that he'd lived.'

Socrates Fortlow has spent twenty-seven years in prison and can kill a man with his bare hands. But now he's out and determined to use his strength for good, to help the downtrodden and oppressed of the Los Angeles ghetto. Tough, tender and wise, Socrates goes to work, running a killer out of town, turning a young man away from a life of crime, restraining himself when the wrong kind of women tempt him.

Like his Greek namesake, Socrates Fortlow asks questions in an attempt to understand his world. His attempt to find morality in poverty and deprivation makes Socrates a modern-day hero.

In this novel of subtle beauty, Walter Mosley shows himself to be the American writer best able to capture the moral ambiguities of the epoch.

Six Easy Pieces

With the love of a good woman and two beautiful children, Easy Rawlins has put his past life of trading favors behind him. Following the loss of his best friend and sidekick, Mouse, he wants to set an example for his children by earning an honest living. But trouble has a way of finding Easy on the mean streets of Watts.

Easy wanders from schoolhouse to whorehouse as he is drawn into investigating the torching of Sojourner Truth, the Junior High School where he works, then the turning over of a local garage and the death of a prostitute. But no man is an island... His job, his lover, his comfortable house and the children he cherishes all count for nothing when the phone rings and a woman asks if he knows where Mouse is. Easy soon discovers that Mouse is as much of a moral challenge dead as alive.

Rich in character and place, the stories reveal the complex nature of the American experience — the issues of class and race, hope and despair, light and darkness. *Six Easy Pieces* is confirmation that Mosley's vision continues to stretch and redefine the American canon.